MARS STATION ALPHA

STEPHEN PENNER

ISBN-13: 978-0-6155747-5-2

ISBN-10: 0-6155747-5-0

Mars Station Alpha

This is a work of fiction. Any similarity with real persons or events is purely coincidental.

MARS
STATION
ALPHA

1

Stanton spied a glint of metal on the horizon of the otherwise barren planetscape.

"We have visual," Commander Mtumbe announced as he steered the *Antares* through the poisonous atmosphere. "Mars Station Alpha."

Mtumbe slid his hand across the control glass, lighting up everyone's personal digital monitor with a magnified image of the space station, overlaid by a data stream from the ship's scanners.

"I see no activity," Petrov observed. "This means no one is alive perhaps?"

"Or it means simply that all shields are working, Aleksandr," countered his fellow Russian, Oksana Rusakova, "and so we cannot see the activity inside."

Mei-Zhu Lin, Stanton's hand-picked tech expert, provided the answer.

"Diagnostics confirm that all shields are on full power," she reported. "We will not see inside with scanners."

Captain John Stanton sat silently in the co-pilot's chair, his eyes fixed on the approaching space station. He had known they wouldn't see anything with scanners. They were going to have to go inside. What he didn't know was why—or what they would find.

"What happened to you in there, Ferguson?" Stanton whispered to himself.

As the ship lurched into its steep descent toward the space station's runway, Lieutenant Nils Dekker, the mission's sole representative of the moribund European Space Agency, pointed out his starboard portal. "What the hell are those?"

"What are what?" asked Petrov.

Stanton finally took his eyes off the station to turn around and see Petrov craning to look out Dekker's side portal.

But before Dekker could answer the Russian, Lin pointed to an indicator light on the ship's instrument panel and announced, "We have received a new communication from Earth."

All eyes turned to Cassandra Gold. A last-minute addition, Gold wasn't even an astronaut. On Earth, she was a Special Agent from the United States Department of State. On Mars—and on the ship—her title was 'Communications Officer.' By direct order of President Akira himself, she outranked even Stanton on all issues of communication with Earth.

Gold pressed a button on the arm of her chair and the message played for everyone. It was President Akira.

"Don't screw this up. The whole planet is watching."

That was it.

Typical, thought Stanton. Akira had just been reelected on his reputation for plain talking—and his promise to get to the bottom of whatever had happened to the Mars colony.

"Shall we send a reply message?" asked Rusakova.

"No," Stanton said simply. "We'd be in the station by the time the message reached Earth. Let's wait till we have something to report."

Then he turned and nodded to Gold. "If that meets with your approval, Agent?"

He still couldn't quite bring himself to call her officer— any type of officer, even Communications Officer.

Gold returned the nod with a curt one of her own. "Approved."

"We should tell him to stop bothering us," joked Dekker, obviously trying to lighten the mood a bit. "We're trying to land a spaceship."

No one laughed.

"I'm the one trying to land this spaceship," Mtumbe snapped. "So everyone just be quiet for a minute. I didn't train to land this thing alone. There was supposed to be a ground crew talking me down."

Stanton stared straight out the cockpit glass again. "The first crew did it without any help, Daniel."

Mtumbe smiled tightly. "I didn't say I couldn't do it. I said I didn't train for it. Now everybody shut up and hold on. We're coming in and I've only got four hundred meters to bring this thing to a complete stop."

His hand flew across the control glass. The landing gear dropped and the wing-flaps pulled up just as the ship reached the ground. The ship slammed into the landing strip and decelerated fast. The crew was thrown forward against their seatbelts. A few more motions over the control glass and the ship's brakes were bringing the 90 tonne spaceship to a bone-shaking halt at the end of the runway.

After a moment, Stanton said, "I knew you could do it."

Mtumbe smiled again, this time more fully. "And I knew you were goading me," he said. "Just doing my assignment. Now let's taxi this baby back to the airlock."

As Mtumbe turned the ship around, Stanton noticed Petrov lean over to Dekker.

"What did you see?" Petrov whispered.

"Well, I'm not exactly sure what it was," Dekker started to reply, but then he looked at Gold, who was making no effort to conceal her eavesdropping. "I'll tell you later, Alex."

Petrov looked over at Gold as well. "Ah, yes," he said. "We will talk to each other later."

Gold rolled her eyes and looked out the ship's windshield. They were approaching the airlock. She grinned.

"I don't know what we'll find inside," she suddenly announced, "and I don't care. Whatever happened in there will remain confidential until and unless I authorize communication back to Command. Understood?"

"What happens on Mars stays on Mars, eh?" joked Dekker.

"Shut up, Dekker," ordered Stanton. Then, addressing Gold, he said, "We all know our roles, Agent. You can stop puffing your chest out at us."

"Although," said Dekker, "you have a very nice—"

"Shut. Up. Dekker," repeated Stanton.

Dekker nodded to Stanton, winked at Gold, and smiled to himself.

"Why don't you all be quiet?" Mtumbe said. The ship had reached the airlock. "I need to line this up perfectly."

Gold glared over at Dekker, but he just made a kissing noise to her.

"Dekker..." warned Stanton.

"*Oui, mon capitan,*" said the Dutchman. "Shutting up."

Mtumbe wiped his brow then unleashed his hands across the control glass once more. The ship jerked and thrust. Then it slowly rolled forward into the airlock. Without so much as a scrape, the nose of the craft pressed into the airlock and a loud pop shook the cockpit. The ship had docked.

"Good job, Commander," Stanton patted him on the shoulder. Then he turned around to address the rest of his crew.

"Eighteen months ago the original Mars colonists began their tour of duty at the first manned space station on another planet, Mars Station Alpha. The world eagerly endured the minutes it took even light-speed communications to travel between the two planets. Even the most routine oxygen farm progress report was thrilling. And it was especially thrilling for us because we were to be the second crew of colonists, set to relieve the first crew when Earth and Mars aligned again."

He looked to Agent Gold. "Present company excepted."

Gold crossed her arms and offered a saccharine smile.

"But as the planets continued their separate orbits," Stanton went on, "and the distance between them grew, we all held our collective breath nine months ago when Mars went behind the sun and communications became impossible. Still, we knew we'd hear all about the latest burnt breakfast, or surprising geological find, or whatever, once Mars swung out from behind the sun. But when it did, there was nothing. No communications at all. And there's been none since.

"Our relief mission has become a rescue mission. Or, God forbid, a recovery mission. For six months we've been stuck in this tiny ship, making our way to Mars, not knowing what we'd find when we got there."

He nodded again to Gold. "So I agree with our late addition: we don't know what we'll find. But I disagree too. I care. I care what happened to that crew and I care what happens to this crew."

It was silent for a moment. Then Dekker said, "Nice speech, Captain."

Before Stanton could respond, Lin announced, "Pressurization has been equalized. We can enter the station now."

With a nod from Stanton, they all unstrapped themselves from their seats, pulled on their helmets, and filed toward the airlock.

"Everyone ready?" Stanton asked over their shared comm link as he placed his hand on the door handle.

"Ready, Captain," answered Mtumbe.

"Ready," added Lin and Rusakova.

Dekker and Petrov each gave a thumbs-up.

Gold stood at the back of the group and didn't respond.

Stanton nodded, took a deep breath, then pressed down on the pressurized hatch handle.

The resultant explosion was deafening, even in the thin Martian air that rushed in through the breeched airlock.

2

"Is everyone all right?!" Stanton's voice filled everyone's helmet comm. He had a different voice in his own head.

That's why you're always second to me, Junior, he could hear Ferguson saying. *You're fine once things are in place, but you're not quite up to leading the advance team.*

"Status report, everyone!" Stanton tried not to sound frantic, but he couldn't see anything. The explosion had knocked out all the lights in the ship.

Lin was the first to respond. "Lin OK," she said simply over the comm link.

"Rusakova good."

"Petrov good."

"Dekker OK," came the Dutchman's voice. "Although I am a bit hungry."

"Mtumbe OK."

Stanton waited a few moments, but Agent Gold didn't check in. He didn't know if she was hurt or just being stubborn.

"Gold?" he said. "Gold, report."

"I'm here, Captain," she said over the comm link. "Perhaps you should worry more about the airlock breech than taking roll."

The carbon dioxide atmosphere had penetrated into and filled the ship, but Stanton knew it wasn't quite the emergency such a hull breech would have been in the vacuum of space. The station had been built in the temperate equatorial region, so daytime temperatures were in the high teens centigrade—sufficiently comfortable. The real problem was that there was no oxygen in the air, just lots and lots of carbon dioxide. But as long as they kept their helmets on, they would have oxygen enough for a few hours.

"Thanks for the advice," Stanton replied. He was too relieved everyone was okay to stay angry over Gold's comment.

"Our first priority is now oxygen," he announced. "Daniel, you stay here with Rusakova and Dekker. Reseal the airlock and evacuate the CO2. Then get the ship's atmosphere back to breathable. Lin, Petrov, and Gold, you come with me into the station. Let's see whether there's any breathable air in there, and if not, whether we can get the oxygen farm up and running in short order."

"We should also figure out what caused the explosion," Gold suggested.

"You may be in charge of communications, Gold," snapped Stanton, "but I'm still the commander of this mission. You can stop trying to direct it."

Gold didn't respond, but her huff was clearly audible over the comm link.

When they reached the end of the airlock Lin examined the door to the station. "This section of airlock is not damaged," she announced.

"Can you tell whether there's breathable air inside?" Stanton asked.

"Negative," replied Lin. "The seal is in tact, but so are the shields. Our scanners can't read through them."

Stanton nodded but was silent as he considered their next step. Whatever had caused the first explosion might cause a second one. They had been fortunate that their spacesuits hadn't been damaged. They might not be that fortunate again.

He put his hand on the airlock's input glass and entered the code the station was supposed to recognize. If all interior systems were in order, the station's computer would initiate the airlock door synchronization necessary to pass through.

Nothing happened.

Stanton decided not to be surprised. He figured there would be plenty to surprise him inside the station. He grabbed a hold of the manual override handles and tried to force Ferguson's mocking laughter from his head as he wondered whether he was about to blow his crew to smithereens.

You're not quite up to leading the advance team.

He pressed down until he could feel the seal giving way. Gold took a few steps back; Lin and Petrov didn't. A low hiss transformed into a satisfying pop and the first of two doors opened without incident.

They entered and closed the door behind them. Once it was closed, a metallic clank signaled the activation of the airlock vents.

"Oxygen levels increasing from zero to seven percent," Petrov read from his scanner. "Eleven percent. Twenty percent. Nitrogen levels also rising.

"Thirty-one percent," he went on, then he looked up at the captain. "Oxygen level stabilizing at forty-three percent. I suppose that's breathable."

"That's too breathable," Stanton frowned. "Ideal level is twenty-one percent."

"Oxygen is combustible in high concentrations," remarked Gold.

Stanton was taken aback by her comment, or rather by that comment coming from her. "How's that again?"

"I'm not just some government bureaucrat," Gold answered. "There's a reason I was selected and approved for this mission. I have more degrees than the rest of you combined and most of them are in the sciences."

"Good to know," Stanton replied, looking over at Petrov. Petrov just offered a shrug. Lin was smiling behind her faceshield, although Stanton wasn't quite sure what she was smiling about.

"Look for carbon," Gold continued. "Any signs of sparking or burning at the airlock handle. It may explain the explosion."

Stanton stared at Gold through his faceplate. But he knew a good idea was a good idea, regardless of its source.

"Mtumbe," he called out over the comm link.

It only took a moment for Mtumbe to respond. "Yes, Captain?"

"We're almost in the station," Stanton reported. "Oxygen levels are grossly elevated, but it's breathable. Once you've repaired the ship, come through to meet us inside."

"Roger that, Captain."

"And Mtumbe?"

"Yes?"

"When you come through," Stanton looked at Gold, "check the doors for signs of sparking or burning."

"Captain?" asked Mtumbe.

"Just a hunch."

Gold frowned and raised an eyebrow at her captain.

"A hypothesis," Stanton corrected. "From Agent Gold."

Mtumbe didn't reply immediately.

"I think she may be right," Stanton added. "So just look for it and let me know what you find."

"Will do, Captain," said Mtumbe. "We should be able to meet you inside within thirty minutes."

"Great," answered Stanton. "Just comm link us when you're inside. Stanton out."

He turned his attention back to the second airlock door. Then, without turning to look back at her, he muttered, "Thanks, Gold."

Gold didn't reply. Stanton figured she'd just use the whole exchange later to her advantage if she could.

"This door should be easier to open," Lin advised the captain. "It is also airtight, but not designed for heavy-duty pressure differences."

Stanton grabbed the manual release latch and pressed down. Sure enough, it opened almost as easily as a regular door. A suction noise, a pop, the slightest whoosh of air, and they were inside Mars Station Alpha.

And by all indications they were alone.

They had stepped into what was designated as the Entry Bay. Like all the rooms on this first permanent residence on another planet, it was tiny. More closet than room. To reinforce that feel, spacesuits hung on pegs along one wall, with attachable boots resting beneath. The opposite wall housed a control glass for the airlocks. Although the power was still fueling the lights and air systems, the control glass was off.

"Lin," Stanton instructed, "try to determine if the control glass was switched off manually or turned off on its own somehow."

Lin offered a quick "Yes, Captain," and set about examining the glass. The control panel offered a humming sound as she powered it back up.

"What's the oxygen level, Petrov?" Stanton asked the cosmonaut over his comm link.

"Still very high," came his reply after he looked down at his scanner. "Forty-one percent."

"I'd like to preserve our personal air supplies," Stanton said. "So let's try breathing this stuff."

Petrov consulted his scanner. "Ambient temperature is nineteen degrees," he advised. "Pleasant enough."

Stanton reached up and released the seal between his helmet and his spacesuit.

"If this goes badly," he said before he lifted his helmet, "Mtumbe is second-in-command. Remember that, Gold."

She offered a tight smile. "Please hurry, Captain," she said. "If you're going to asphyxiate, I'd like to get on with it."

Stanton couldn't help but smile at that himself. Ferguson hadn't had to deal with a bitchy bureaucrat.

He lifted his helmet a few centimeters and carefully inhaled through his nose.

More importantly, after a moment he exhaled again.

"Smells weird," he announced. "Stale and sweet and musty and metallic, all at the same time. But it's breathable."

Petrov quickly released his own helmet and set it aside. "I have never liked wearing helmets," he explained. "They make me feel trapped just a little bit."

Gold removed her helmet as well, but without comment, and placed it under her arm. Stanton was struck at how shiny and bright her long, blonde hair was. It was easy to forget how physically attractive she was when she opened her bitter and caustic mouth.

Lin had already removed her helmet and was busy entering commands into the entry bay's control glass.

"I am starting to get a headache," Petrov said, raising a gloved hand to his forehead. "The oxygen level perhaps?"

"The oxygen level for sure," Stanton answered. "It's called oxygen intoxication. Be careful. In addition to headaches, we're also going to feel a burst of energy from the extra O2. Resist the urge to run ahead and do cartwheels."

"I'm not really a cartwheel girl," Gold offered.

Stanton smiled at her and raised an eyebrow. "What kind of girl are you?"

He instantly regretted the comment. He told himself it was the extra oxygen.

"Sorry, Gold," he harrumphed and shook his head. "No offense meant. Um, we really need to get the oxygen levels down. Let's survey the oxygen farm on our way to the control room."

Lin looked up from the control glass. "I haven't figured out yet how this was powered down, but I think I need only a few more minutes."

"Fine," said Stanton. "You stay here. Petrov, Gold, come with me to the station's control room."

Part of him questioned leaving anyone alone at this

point, but things seemed reasonably under control. They could breathe at least, although he too was getting a headache. Still, he didn't want to be an over reactive, overprotective nanny of a captain. Lin was a tough, experienced sinonaut. She had weathered the six-month space voyage without incident. She could certainly handle a few minutes examining a control glass by herself.

Petrov, Gold, and Stanton exited into the long hallway that connected all the chambers and rooms of the station. The first room they came too was essentially an attached greenhouse. It housed a variety of thick green plants from Earth, all breathing deeply of Mars' carbon dioxide atmosphere, and—more importantly to Stanton and his crew—exhaling pure oxygen.

"The oxygen farm is thriving," Petrov observed. "That explains the high oxygen levels."

"It also suggests there are no colonists here," Stanton opined. "The farm was designed to produce the right amount of oxygen for seven humans to breathe and exhale as CO_2. Without them, the oxygen level will just keep rising. So we know they haven't been here for a while."

"Or they are here," Gold corrected, "but they haven't been breathing for a while."

Stanton greeted that unpleasant, but accurate, assessment with a stone countenance. "Let's get to the control room," he said.

The only other thing they passed on the way to the control room was a row of thick windows facing west, offering a view of the coming Martian sunset. The landscape was turning a deep amber as the sun dipped toward the horizon.

The control room was too small for all three of them, so

Gold volunteered to wait in the hallway. These control panels were still up and running. They confirmed that the oxygen levels were above forty percent.

"The good news is that the oxygen farm is doing quite well," said Petrov as he pulled up various charts and readings. "The bad news is, as we know, there appears to be nothing to offset the oxygen production."

"Can we adjust it manually?" Stanton suggested.

Petrov considered. "I think so. We just need a way to decrease the relative oxygen level."

"What's the best way to do that, do you think?" asked Stanton.

"How about you open a window?" snarked Gold, pointing out at the planet full of carbon dioxide.

Petrov laughed. "Basically she is correct, Captain. Nitrogen would be better, but we can open some external vents and let in enough carbon dioxide to reduce the oxygen concentration. At least until things stabilize with our presence here now."

"Great," said Stanton. "You work on that. Gold, come with me."

"Am I going to the principal's office?" she quipped.

Stanton forced out the inappropriate thought that had unexpectedly popped into his head. "No, Agent Gold. We're going to the crew's quarters. If they're here but not breathing, as you so sensitively put it, it's likely we'll find them there."

Gold couldn't suppress a wince. Stanton saw it.

"What's wrong, Agent?" he teased. "No degree in mortuary sciences?"

"Go to hell, Captain," she said cheerily, pushing past him toward the quarters.

Go to hell, Stanton considered. He looked around the abandoned space station and couldn't help but wonder if maybe he had.

Any concerns about whether they might find seven dead astronauts were quickly dispelled. All of the quarters were empty. Stanton remembered learning that there had been some discussion about one large sleeping room, or one male and one female, but eventually it was decided that eighteen months on a barren rock was a long time to go without any privacy. So the residential wing of the station consisted of seven separate sleeping rooms, each barely larger than the cot inside, plus a communal kitchen and eating area.

Each sleeping room was in perfect, inspection-ready order: the beds made tightly, the drawers and closet full of clean, folded clothes, the computer stations turned off and folded up. Stanton thought it looked like an advertisement for the first hotel on Mars. But even though the furniture was ready for the next guest, all of the colonists' personal effects remained. Posters taped to the walls. Drawings and letters from children. Photographs of friends and family, favorite places and cherished memories.

Stanton walked into one of the quarters and examined a photograph of astro-colonist Brigid Osterhafn with her two young children at some crowded European beach.

'We're proud of you, Mommy,' was written at the bottom corner of the image.

"It's like they knew they were leaving," Stanton said, still examining the photo, "but they couldn't take anything with them."

Stanton was about to look for Ferguson's cabin when Mtumbe came over the comm link.

"Captain," he said. "Come back to the control room. Quick."

Stanton looked at Gold, who returned his look of concern with one of indifference.

"Glad you made it inside, Daniel," he said. "What's the problem?"

"Just come back. You'll see."

Mtumbe was clearly upset, unusual for him.

Stanton hurried through the narrow walkway from the crew's quarters to the control panel. Gold trudged behind him. Mtumbe was standing outside the room, with Dekker and Rusakova behind him, and Petrov and Lin peering out from within.

"Okay," Stanton asked as he walked up, "what's going on?"

Mtumbe didn't say anything, but instead pointed to a support beam directly across from the control room. Carved into the plastic coating, exposing the steel underneath, was a single word:

'CROATOAN'

3

"Croatoan," Stanton read the word aloud. "Why is that familiar?"

"Perhaps it's Martian?" Dekker suggested. "Maybe it means 'No Vacancy.'"

"No," said Mtumbe. "It's Native American."

That stunned everyone into silence for a moment.

Finally Dekker asked, "There are Native Americans on Mars?"

Stanton turned to the Dutchman. "Shut up, Lieutenant." When Dekker opened his mouth to protest, Stanton added, "That's an order."

Stanton turned his attention back to Mtumbe. "Now I know why that's familiar."

Gold nodded too, but didn't say anything.

"Well, I do not," said Rusakova. "Please explain, Commander."

"Croatoan was the name of a Native American tribe in Virginia," answered Mtumbe. "The ones who lived near the lost colony of Roanoke."

"Roanoke?" repeated Dekker.

"L— Lost?" asked Petrov.

"Yeah, lost." Mtumbe frowned as he tried to remember his history lessons. "It was one of the first English colonies in North America, established in 1564. But the next year war broke out between Britain and Spain and all available British ships were commandeered to fight the Spanish Armada. No supply ships could get to the Roanoke colony for three years."

"Three years?" confirmed Rusakova. "That is twice what our comrades on Mars faced."

"Right," agreed Mtumbe. "When a British supply ship finally arrived in 1568, the colony was gone. The buildings had all been carefully dismantled and removed. The only clue was the word 'Croatoan' carved into a nearby tree."

"So what happened to the colony?" Petrov demanded.

"No one knows," Mtumbe answered. "Some people think they starved, some think they were killed by the Native Americans, and some even say they were taken by ghosts."

"Ghosts?" scoffed Lin.

Petrov also asked, "Ghosts?" but his tone was one of fear, not doubt.

"Ghosts," grinned Mtumbe. "The colony had been built on top of an Indian burial ground."

Dekker leaned over to Petrov and whispered something in his ear. Petrov's eyes widened and he looked at Dekker, who nodded earnestly. Stanton could see things were getting out of hand.

"Okay, okay," Stanton stepped in to regain control. "Enough with the ghost stories."

He looked at the word carved into the space station wall and frowned. "Obviously this is some effort by the first crew to communicate with us. There are no Native American tribes on Mars, so it can't mean they've left to join one."

He frowned, not sure what to do. He was glad Ferguson wasn't there to see his indecision.

"Daniel," he asked finally, "did the explosion damage the ship's communications system?"

Gold visibly bristled at even the suggestion of sending a comm back to Earth. But before she could object, Mtumbe replied, "It shorted out a bunch of the systems, including communications. I'm pretty sure they'll be okay, but I had to reboot them. We won't know for a few hours."

"Let's check out the station's comm center," Stanton decided. Then, he regarded Petrov and the carved word. "All together."

Gold finally spoke up. "Why the comm center, Captain?"

Stanton stared at her for a moment.

"Two reasons," he replied tensely. "One: to see if the comm system is working. And two: if it is, to comm back to Earth."

"No objection to number one," Gold said calmly, "but I'm vetoing number two."

Stanton didn't say anything, but only because he didn't get the chance.

"What?" demanded Petrov. "Of course we must inform them of what we have found!"

"We don't know what we've found," Gold retorted. "At least not yet."

"We have found no crew and a disturbing message," pressed Petrov. Then he looked at Dekker. "Plus—"

But Dekker elbowed him and he stopped.

Gold narrowed her eyes at the Russian. "Plus what?"

"Yes, Alex," pressed Rusakova. "Plus what?"

"Plus nothing," Petrov replied, before crossing his arms and whispering something to Dekker.

Gold's eyes flared. "There will be no secrets on this mission," she declared.

"Yet you wish to keep what we have discovered secret from those on Earth," observed Lin.

"That's not keeping secrets," argued Gold. "That's information management."

Stanton considered joining the argument, but his crew was doing fine without him.

"You can call it what you like," Rusakova said, "but it amounts to the same thing: censorship."

Gold took a deep breath. "So you want to tell the entire world that the colonists are missing and the only clue is a Native American word that was carved into a tree six hundred years ago?"

"Er... yes?" tried Dekker as the others fell silent.

"Do you have any idea what kind of a panic that could start?" Gold demanded. "Everyone would start predicting the end of the world. And how would it make the colonists' families feel? Shouldn't we wait to report back until we better understand what there is to report?"

The crew looked down and around, but no one said anything.

Finally, Mtumbe looked to Stanton. "Captain?"

Gold looked at him too. Her eyes seemed to challenge him to defy her.

"It's not like we're contacting the media," he soothed. "We're going to tell our government. They can decide whether to disseminate the information further."

Gold's eyes narrowed to slits. "I have command authority over all communication issues," she hissed.

"I know, I know," Stanton waved a hand toward her and turned away. "First thing's first. Let's go find the comm center."

Gold grabbed Stanton's arm as the others filed out toward the comm center. "Captain, I need to speak with you."

"It can wait," Stanton replied.

"No it can't," Gold insisted. "You need to hear what I have to say."

"No, Agent Gold," Stanton snapped. "You need to listen to what I have to say. You may have been added to this mission by the President himself, but you are just another member of my crew. I am the captain of the ship and the commander of this mission. I was willing to play along with the 'Gold has jurisdiction over communications' charade, but only so long as it didn't endanger anyone's life."

"You need to respect my authority in front of the rest of the crew," Gold complained.

"I should say the same to you," Stanton countered. "If you have as many degrees as you think you do, then maybe somewhere along the way you learned that once a ship has left port, and circumstances and situations are subject to sudden, unexpected changes, the captain—that's me—the captain has final and absolute authority over all matters."

Gold blinked at him.

"Including communications," Stanton added just to make sure she understood. "I have six crew members to protect from our ship, plus seven more to rescue. That's thirteen lives in my hands alone. You will respect that."

Gold's full lips tightened into a thin line.

"Now I'm confronted with an abandoned space station and a cryptic clue referencing a six hundred year old lost colony eaten by ghosts. I'll give you the chance to authorize my communication to Earth so the rest of the crew still thinks you're calling those shots, but I am making that communication."

Gold stared back with cold green eyes. They almost betrayed some emotion, but she stopped it. Then she looked down.

"Don't send that communication, Captain," she said quietly.

Stanton stood up straight and crossed his arms.

"Give me one good reason why not," he challenged.

Gold looked up again and met his gaze softly with those same green eyes. "Because I'm the one who carved 'Croatoan' into the post."

4

"What?!" Stanton was incredulous. "You carved it?"

Gold gave a hesitant nod.

"Why on Earth would you do that?" demanded Stanton.

"Hey, you just made a joke," Gold pointed out. "You should have said 'Why on *Mars* would you do that?'"

Stanton didn't laugh. He just stared intently at her. "Why, Gold?"

Gold shrugged and offered a sigh. "It was test."

"A test?" repeated Stanton. "A test of what? What the hell were you trying to test?"

"You," answered Gold. "And your crew."

Stanton shook his head. "How does carving Croatoan into the wall test me or my crew?"

"Look at how you all reacted," said Gold. "Some outlandish message that can't possibly be real, and you're ready to report back to Earth that Mars Station Alpha is haunted by ghosts of a lost Native American tribe."

"I think you're exaggerating a bit," Stanton answered after a moment.

Gold smiled. A full but cold smile. "Maybe," she admitted. "But I think I proved my point. You need someone to check your impulse to ask for help."

Stanton winced. That hit a little bit too close to home.

The reason I always go first, Ferguson had once told him, *is that you're always waiting to call for back up. When they need someone to go where there is no back up, they send me. Once I've established the beachhead, then you can come. You're great at logistics, Junior, but you're no pioneer.*

Stanton took a deep breath and shook the evil cobwebs from his head. "You'll need to tell the crew," he announced. "They're not going to be happy."

Gold's eyes widened. "Tell them I carved it?"

"Of course," Stanton confirmed. "You scared them half to death, especially Petrov. He's ready to call for an exorcism."

Gold shifted her weight. "Um, that is..." She smiled again, softly, and stepped next to Stanton. "Can't this just be our little secret?" she breathed in his ear.

Stanton was flustered, aroused, puzzled, and angered all at the same time. He was pretty sure he was in charge of the conversation when they'd started, but now he couldn't even remember what they were talking about.

"A-hem. Cough. Cough." Mtumbe walked up behind them. "Hope I'm not interrupting anything."

Stanton jumped away from Gold, practically pushing her away.

"No, no, no," insisted Stanton. "Of course not. We were just, that is, um... Agent Gold has something to tell you, something to tell everyone. Isn't that right, Agent Gold?"

Gold smiled at Stanton. "Whatever you say, Captain," she purred as she pushed past him, much closer than necessary, toward the comm center.

Mtumbe, who had to move into the control room to let Gold pass by, stepped out again and raised an inquiring eyebrow at Stanton.

"Don't ask, Daniel," Stanton raised his hand at him. "Because I don't know either."

Mtumbe laughed and slapped his captain on the back as they headed toward the comm center. "Well, we've got something to tell you too."

"What is it?" Stanton asked.

"Oh, it will wait until we get to the comm center. I can't wait to hear Gold's announcement."

He paused, then ventured. "You two engaged now?"

Stanton didn't turn around. "Not funny, Daniel."

Mtumbe smiled. "Pretty sure it was."

When they reached the comm center Petrov was practically yelling at Gold. "What is it? What is so important?"

When Stanton and Mtumbe arrived, Petrov complained to his captain, "She said she has announcement but she wouldn't tell us until you got here. So what is it? What is going on?"

"Aleksandr," soothed Rusakova, "Calm down. Everything is going to be all right."

"All right?" Petrov scoffed. "We are trapped on another planet, the crew before us is missing, and the only clue we find tells us that the station is haunted! How can you say we will be all right?"

Stanton could see Petrov was losing it. He felt the strain of his position again. He knew part of achieving a successful mission was keeping everyone from going insane in the cramped quarters of space. Gold's little stunt hadn't helped matters.

"Don't worry, Alex," Stanton said, "I think you'll feel better after you hear what Agent Gold has to say."

Petrov threw a wild-eyed stare at Gold, who just shrugged diffidently.

"I carved that word into the wall," she said, "to see how you all would react. I thought you might rush here and try to communicate with Earth about something you hadn't fully verified."

Stanton caught a glimpse of Lin, who seemed to smile, but the rest of the crew was livid.

"How could you do that?" Rusakova demanded.

"What the hell is wrong with you?" fumed Dekker.

Petrov just stared at her, chest heaving and fists clenched. Stanton stepped closer in case Petrov leapt at her.

"It just proves that you need to trust me when it comes to communication issues," Gold smirked.

"Trust you?" Petrov laughed. "I have never trusted you. And now I never will trust you."

Gold tossed a hand in the air. "Fine." Then she turned to Stanton. "In any case, there's no need to comm back to Earth about this, although I suppose a standard status report is due. Just so they know we made it inside."

Mtumbe finally spoke up. "And that's what we have to tell you." He pointed at the multiple control glasses in the comm center. "The comm system doesn't work. All the controls are in perfect order, but our communications won't send. We've gone completely dark."

No calling home now, Junior.

5

"Why isn't it working?" Stanton asked.

"The control glasses are in perfect order," Lin reported. "They respond to our commands, but we cannot obtain a signal."

Stanton turned to his crew. "Any ideas?"

"The external equipment," Rusakova answered. "If the internal equipment is working, then it must be the external equipment which is not working."

Stanton nodded and turned to Gold. "Agent Gold, you're our communications expert. Do you agree with Rusakova?"

Gold hesitated. "I'm not really hardware. I'm more content."

"You have no degree in electromagnetic radiation?" Petrov teased.

"Fine." Gold crossed her arms. "I'll agree with Rusakova. If the interior systems are working, it only makes sense that the exterior systems have failed."

Stanton smiled. "I'm glad you agree. You can come with Lin, Mtumbe, and me up on the roof."

"The roof?" Gold repeated.

"The communication antenna array is on the roof," Stanton explained. "We need to check it out, so I want our communications officer with us."

"Of course, Captain," answered Gold sweetly after a moment. "Glad to offer my expertise."

Stanton thought for a moment. "We'll need to change into heavy duty suits. These travel suits are fine for potential breathing issues inside the station, but I don't want to be up on the roof without proper protection."

"We could use the ones from the entry bay," Mtumbe suggested.

"Have we inspected them?" Dekker asked.

"Not yet," replied Stanton. "But we can do a preliminary inspection before venturing outside. It's not like we're venturing far afield. If there are any issues, we'll only be seconds away from reentry into the station."

Stanton knew it was risky, but he hoped his expression didn't betray his thoughts. He looked out the window at the coming sunset. The day had been warm enough but the thin Martian atmosphere wouldn't hold the heat like Earth's thick clouds.

"If we don't do this now, we'll have to wait until morning," he thought aloud. "And I don't want to wait until morning."

Ferguson wouldn't have hesitated to head out with the station's uninspected spacesuits, Stanton knew. On the other hand, where was Ferguson now?

6

"Okay, here's what we'll do," Stanton decided. "Lin, Mtumbe, and Gold: you each select a suit and inspect it. If it appears to be in working order, then it will be reinspected by Dekker, Petrov, and Rusakova."

"Who will reinspect your suit, Captain?" asked Lin.

"I'll take care of my own suit," he smiled. "Once the suits are ready, the out-team will exit via the west entrance and climb up the service ladder to the roof. Petrov, you stay at the entrance and monitor our communications at all times. If there's a problem, I want you to know it as soon as it develops."

"Yes, Captain," answered Petrov.

"Rusakova," Stanton went on, "you stay in the comm center to see if we can get the comm up and running again. Assuming we can fix whatever's wrong, we'll need you to confirm communications are working before we come down again."

"Yes, Captain," answered Rusakova.

"And Dekker?" Stanton said.

"Yes, Captain?"

"You climb the interior ladder by the crew's quarters, and station yourself directly below the emergency hatch on the roof. If we need to get inside quickly, blow the hatch so we can get in."

"Won't that let the Martian atmosphere inside?" Dekker questioned.

"Yes," explained Stanton, "but the station is designed to autoseal sections that are breeched. Once the hatch is closed again, the station will vacate the CO_2 and vent in breathable air. So wear your helmet. If we have to do that, it will take a while for the air to be breathable again."

"May I also suggest," Lin added, "that Dekker carry a portable breathing mask for us. If we are entering under an emergency, it may be because one of our suits has failed."

"Good idea," Stanton agreed. Then he added, "Thank you, Commander Lin."

Lin smiled and nodded.

"Does everyone understand their assignments?" Stanton asked.

"Yes, sir," answered Lin and the others. Even Gold offered a "Yes," although she left off the 'sir.'

They made their way back to the entry bay. As they passed the 'CROATOAN' carved in the wall, Dekker slapped Gold on the back.

"Good one, Cassandra," he said jocularly. "You really had Aleksandr going there for a while."

Gold scowled at him for a moment, then her expression softened. "Yes, right. Well, just seeing how everyone would react."

Then she pushed Dekker's hand off of her. "But please don't call me Cassandra. We're crewmates, not friends."

Dekker kept his smile, but it weakened, and Gold walked ahead.

A few minutes later, Stanton, Mtumbe, Lin, and Gold were each inspecting a heavy duty suit. Stanton saw no obvious signs of damage. In fact, like everything else on the ship thus far, they appeared to be inspection-ready. It seemed to Stanton as if the first crew had known they wouldn't be coming back and wanted to leave everything in perfect condition for the next crew.

Following reinspection by the rest of the crew, Stanton and the out-team were ready to exit the station and enter the Martian atmosphere. Lin, Dekker, and Petrov took their stations.

"Comm link check," Stanton said into his helmet comm microphone after the suit was sealed shut. "All parties report."

"Dekker in position beneath emergency hatch," said the Dutchman. "Ladder is uncomfortable."

"Rusakova in position at the comm center control glass," reported the Russian.

"Petrov right here," he said, standing next to the out-team by the airlock to the west entrance. "And I will stay here until your safe return."

"Mtumbe?" Stanton tested, raising a gloved hand toward his second-in-command.

"I can hear you, Captain," Mtumbe replied.

"As can I, Captain," added Lin.

Gold didn't say anything. She was looking out at the desolate Martian landscape.

"Gold?" Stanton said. "Gold?"

Gold turned back with a start. "Yes, yes. I'm here," she said hurriedly.

"Are you all right?" Stanton asked, genuinely concerned. He didn't need someone freaking out once they got outside.

"Of course," snapped Gold. "I'm fine. Let's go."

Stanton and the others entered the airlock, and Petrov sealed the door behind them. A few keypad commands later and the outer door opened, allowing the pale, pink light of the Martian evening to spill into the airlock.

"The roof access ladder is just a few meters around to the left," Stanton announced over the comm link.

Mtumbe led the group toward the ladder. Their steps were slow and large in the considerably weaker gravity of Mars. Inside the station, the gravity had seemed normal enough, especially after six months of weightlessness, but seeing the orange dust they kicked up fall back to the ground in slow motion reminded Stanton just how far they were from home.

Mtumbe was the first go up, followed by Lin, Gold, and finally the captain. He felt like he should pull up the rear for some reason. As he climbed up behind Gold he couldn't help but stare at her bottom even in the heavy duty spacesuit. He made a mental note to check those oxygen levels again.

His thoughts were interrupted about halfway up, though, by Mtumbe's voice over the comm link. Looking past Gold, Stanton could see Lin climbing off the ladder. Mtumbe was already on the roof.

"I don't believe it," Mtumbe said. "I don't fucking believe it."

7

"What is it?" Stanton demanded as he tried to hurry up the ladder. But Gold's behind—attractive or not—was still in his way.

"You'll see when you get up here," Mtumbe replied simply.

Sure enough Gold crested the ladder and Stanton hurried after her. When he surveyed the roof, he understood.

"Well, crap," he said.

The antenna arrays weren't broken. They were gone. Completely, totally, absolutely gone; and not 'broken and knocked off by meteorites' gone. All six of the ten-meter tall arrays, and their accompanying power boxes and attachment hardware, had been carefully dismantled and removed. Communications would be impossible from the station.

"What the hell is going on?" Stanton asked no one in particular. "Did they just pack up and move to Saturn or something?"

"Saturn is gaseous," Lin answered. "They wouldn't be able to go there. A moon perhaps..."

Stanton glared at her. "Thank you, Lieutenant. I'm just

getting frustrated by all this. It makes no sense."

He walked over to where one of the arrays had been connected to the station roof, while Gold walked to the edge to watch the Martian sunset begin in earnest.

"What do you make of this, Gold?" Stanton asked looking over at her.

"What do I make of what?" she replied without turning around.

Stanton sighed. "Just come over here and look at this coupling," he said.

Gold took a few moments to pull her gaze from the sunset and walk over to the captain. "Looks like the antenna is gone," she observed.

"This is serious, Gold," Stanton chided. "I'm curious what your opinion is. You and President Akira seem to have expected some strangeness to have to censor. Well, this is strange, and it's communications, so it would seem to fall under your jurisdiction."

Gold just shrugged.

"Well, you may have carved that stupid joke in the wall down there," Stanton said, "but I know you didn't haul off these antennas. That means something happened here before we arrived. If it happened nine months ago, it would explain the loss of communications from the colony."

Gold turned back to the deepening sunset. "Why would anyone ever want to come here?" she asked. "And why would they ever want to leave?"

Stanton stood up and looked at Gold faceplate to faceplate. "What are you babbling about, Gold?"

She locked eyes with him. "Call me Cassie."

"Are you okay, Gold?" Stanton asked. "You're not

acting like yourself."

"I don't feel like myself," Gold giggled.

Before they could say more, Petrov's shriek pierced everyone's comm link. "Aaaaaayeeeeeeeeee! Aaaaah! Aaaaaaah!"

"Petrov!" Stanton shouted into his comm link. "Petrov! Come in! What is it? What's happening?"

But Petrov just kept screaming like a little girl.

Stanton motioned to Mtumbe and Lin. "Down the ladder. Now."

The three of them rushed to the edge of the roof. Lin hopped down first, followed by Mtumbe. Stanton turned to see where Gold was. She was just standing there.

He hurried back and grabbed her by the shoulders. She didn't resist and he was able to steer her to the ladder. She started down and he followed after her just as Lin reached the ground. But Gold practically slid down the ladder, smashing into Mtumbe as he was nearing the bottom. He fell the last few rungs, his leg getting caught in the steel ladder.

"Damn it!" he yelled as he hit the ground, his leg tangled in the ladder above him.

Gold stumbled aside and Stanton knelt down next to his friend. He could clearly see Mtumbe's bleeding shin through the torn spacesuit.

"Oh, shit," said Mtumbe.

And the poisonous Martian air rushed toward his lungs.

8

"Damn it," said Mtumbe as he tried to seal his torn suit with his hands. He started coughing as the carbon dioxide filled his helmet.

Stanton pulled Mtumbe's leg out of the ladder rungs.

"Stop talking!" he ordered his second-in-command. Then he leaned him forward and grabbed onto the manual air controls on the back of his spacesuit. He opened the valve all the way, blowing oxygen-rich air into Mtumbe's helmet.

"There's only enough air for about two minutes of that," Stanton announced. "Daniel, breathe slowly and shallowly. Lin and Gold, help me pick him up."

Lin rushed to pick up her wounded comrade, but Gold was still lingering at the edge of the scene.

"Gold!" Stanton yelled, but he got no reply.

"Cassie," he tried.

Gold looked over at him. "Yes?"

"Help me carry Daniel inside," he said calmly. "Please."

"Okay, John," she replied and finally stepped over to help.

Mtumbe was coughing and gasping at the oxygen

blowing past his mouth, but he was still conscious. When they lifted him up, he cried out at his leg being touched.

"Quiet, Daniel," Stanton ordered. "Save your breath."

They hurried him to the airlock, but when they got there, Petrov was nowhere to be seen.

"Petrov!" Stanton called out over the comm link. "Petrov!"

But there was no reply.

"Dekker? Rusakova?" he tried. "Can anyone hear me?"

"Yes," came Dekker's reply, followed immediately by Rusakova's, "Yes, sir."

"Abandon your stations and come to the west airlock," Stanton ordered. "Mtumbe is asphyxiating. We need to get inside now."

Mtumbe's coughing was transforming into labored gasping as the air from his suit began to run out and the carbon dioxide once again filled his helmet.

Lin dropped her hold of Mtumbe's injured leg, causing another pain cry, and ran over to the airlock. Stanton watched hopefully as Lin began entering commands into the small glass.

"Come on, Lin," he whispered. Then, "Hold on, Daniel."

Stanton tried to shake the feeling that Ferguson was watching him and laughing. He felt ashamed of even thinking about that while his friend and crewmate was dying in his very arms.

The airlock door flew open, but it wasn't Lin's doing.

"Hurry!" called out Rusakova. She was at the other end of the airlock, ready to pump oxygen into the chamber once they were inside.

Stanton and Gold rushed Mtumbe into the airlock. Or rather, Stanton rushed into the airlock, and Gold trailed behind, barely managing to hold onto Mtumbe's uninjured leg. Lin raced in after them and Rusakova sent the outer door flying shut. Oxygen-rich air flooded the airlock.

But Mtumbe had already stopped breathing.

"No!" shouted Stanton even as they lowered Mtumbe to the floor. "No, Daniel. You're not getting out of this mission that easily."

Stanton yanked off Mtumbe's helmet, then his own. He blew into Mtumbe's mouth and started chest compressions. Without having to be told to do so, Lin replaced Stanton at Mtumbe's head and blew air into Mtumbe's lungs after every third chest compression.

Gold just stood there. She didn't even take off her helmet, but Stanton noticed her start shaking her head.

"Come on, Daniel," Stanton urged as he continued the chest pumps.

The airlock finally reached the proper atmospheric levels and the door to the station opened. Rusakova ran in with the station's ventrofibrillator. She pushed the tube into Mtumbe's throat and laid the stimulator pad on his chest. Stanton and Lin moved away as Rusakova activated the machine.

A loud electric crackle filled the airlock.

Immediately Mtumbe began coughing violently. He thrashed a bit and Rusakova removed the tube from his mouth. Mtumbe coughed again and again, deeper and deeper, as his lungs expelled the carbon dioxide and filled themselves the oxygen-rich air of the station.

Stanton reached out and grabbed a hold of Lin's and

Rusakova's hands. "Good job," he said. "Thank you."

Gold shifted her weight, then started to unseal her helmet.

Dekker came running in just as Mtumbe started sitting up, still coughing but clearly going to survive.

"What happened out there?" Dekker asked.

Stanton and Lin both looked at Gold.

"I slipped," Mtumbe managed to rasp.

Gold shook her head. "No, what happened is, I spaced out and slipped on the ladder above Commander Mtumbe. I slid down into him, causing him to injure his leg and tear his suit."

Stanton suppressed a smile. He had expected less from her.

"I don't know what happened to me out there," Gold continued. She shook her head. "I don't know. I— I'm sorry."

"We can sort out whose fault it was later," Stanton said. "Right now we have two more important dilemmas."

"What are those?" asked Dekker.

"First, attending to Mtumbe's leg," Stanton replied. "And second, where the hell is Petrov?"

9

Petrov had abandoned his post. Worse yet, by doing so, he had endangered the lives of his fellow crew members. Worst of all, it had been his shrieking that had sent them speeding down the ladder in the first place.

Stanton and Dekker lifted Mtumbe and carefully carried him into the airlock control bay.

"Water," Mtumbe whispered and pointed to his throat as they set him on the floor.

Stanton nodded to Dekker and the Dutchman ran toward the commissary.

"Petrov," Stanton said firmly into the comm link. "Status report."

There was no reply.

"Lin, can you locate him by his comm signature?" Stanton requested.

Lin cocked her head at him. "Captain?" she asked.

Stanton mouthed 'Say yes.' He had to do it a second time before she gave an exaggerated nod. He knew they couldn't really do that, but he figured Petrov didn't know it.

"Ah, yes, Captain," Lin announced into the comm link in her suit collar. "I will do that right now, Captain. It will tell us exactly where Lieutenant Petrov is."

Then they all stood there and waited.

After a moment came Petrov's voice, thin and weak. "I'm on the ship," he said. "Back on the ship."

Stanton nodded thanks to Lin. Mtumbe tried to say something, but it only made him cough some more.

"Why are you on the ship, Petrov?" Stanton demanded.

He didn't reply.

"Petrov?" Stanton followed up, but again no reply.

"Aleksandr," Rusakova soothed over the shared comm link, "why are you on the ship?"

After a moment, Petrov replied, "You may come aboard, Oksana."

Stanton looked again to the others, then held a finger to his lips and turned off his comm link. The rest followed suit, except that when Rusakova went to turn his off, Stanton stopped her.

"Tell him you're on your way," he whispered directly into her ear so even the sensitive comm link wouldn't pick it up. "We'll follow behind."

Rusakova nodded. "I am coming, Aleksandr," she said into her comm link.

There was a long pause, then Petrov groaned, "Good."

Stanton instructed Rusakova to walk to the entry bay and wait there for him. She left and Stanton turned his attention to rest of his crew. "Daniel, are you okay?"

Mtumbe raised a still gloved thumbs up. "I'll be fine," he assured in a raspy voice. "Just need a chance to rest up."

"Good," said Stanton. Then he instructed, "Lin and

Dekker, you stay here with Mtumbe. Gold, you come with me."

"Me?" protested Gold. "Why me?"

"Well, I'm guessing," explained Stanton, "Daniel doesn't really want to hang out with you right now."

Gold looked at Mtumbe, but he averted his eyes. He reached down and squeezed his injured leg, almost at her, but that smile of his couldn't be fully repressed.

"Fine," huffed Gold. She stormed past the captain toward the entry bay.

"We'll be right back," Stanton said to the remaining crew with a smile. "Everything will be just fine. Really."

Mtumbe shrugged. Dekker looked like he was trying to think of something funny to say. Lin just nodded and replied, "Yes, sir."

Stanton caught up with Gold about half way to the ship.

"Are you okay?" he asked.

"I'm fine," she snapped.

"You were a little out of it up on the roof."

"I'm not sure what you mean, Captain," Gold replied as she kept walking, looking straight down the walkway and not at Stanton.

Stanton considered for a moment.

"You told me to call you Cassie."

Gold stopped walking. "No, I didn't," she said sharply.

"Yes, actually, you did."

"I would never have said that," Gold insisted. "No one calls me Cassie. My father called me Cassie when I was a little girl."

"Oh well, that's nice," said Stanton, unsure what else to

say.

"No, it's not," rebuked Gold. "Don't call me Cassie. Don't ever call me Cassie."

She stormed off again to the entry bay.

When Stanton walked in behind her, Rusakova was already waiting by the airlock door. Stanton gave her a nod to go ahead.

"Aleksandr," Rusakova said softly into her comm link. "We are here."

This time Petrov's reply was quick, "We? Who is with you, Oksana?"

"It is only the captain, Aleksandr," answered Rusakova, "and Agent Gold."

"No!" yelled Petrov, so loud Rusakova winced. "Not Gold. I heard what happened to her up on the roof. I heard it all. She cannot come in. Not her. No, no, no. She cannot."

Gold started to protest, but Stanton put up a hand to stop her. Then he turned his comm link back on. "Okay, Petrov. Gold will stay out here. Rusakova and I are coming on board."

There was a pause, then Petrov said, "All right, Captain. Thank you. Yes, Captain, just you and Oksana. Thank you."

Stanton ordered Gold to wait in the entry bay, then he activated the airlocks and he and Rusakova passed through to the ship.

Inside, the ship was mostly dark; just a few of the small, overhead lights were on. More noticeably, though, the air smelled and felt better. Stanton had gotten used to the high oxygen levels on the station. They hadn't gotten around to fixing that yet either.

"Petrov?" called Stanton.

"Aleksandr?" tried Rusakova.

"I am here, Oksana." Petrov raised his hand and they could see him slumped into one of the seats in the back row of the cockpit.

"Are you all right, Aleksandr?" Rusakova walked slowly toward him. Stanton stayed back by the door.

Petrov sighed deeply. "Yes, Oksana. I am all right."

When Rusakova reached him she took a hold of his chin and gently raised his face. "Why, Aleksandr. You look like you've seen a ghost?"

Petrov smiled weakly. "Yes, Oksana. I have."

10

"What are you talking about, Petrov?" Stanton barked. It was bad enough the original crew was missing without a trace, he didn't want to deal with a schizophrenic communications officers and a hallucinating cosmonaut.

Having fun yet, Junior? Ferguson's laughter practically echoed in his skull.

"I am talking about ghosts, Captain," Petrov answered calmly. The few overhead lights cast deep shadows over his eyes and mouth. "Do you not believe in ghosts?"

Stanton avoided the general question for a more specific one. "I don't believe in ghosts on Mars."

"Where there has been life, there can be ghosts," Petrov replied.

"Aleksandr," Rusakova asked, "why are you talking this way? Whatever has upset you, surely it was not a ghost. A shadow perhaps, or something equally innocent."

"Oh, Oksana, you do not understand." Petrov reached up and touched her face gently. "You are from Moscow, but I from a small village in the Caucasus. The spirits are still strong there. My grandmother could see them."

"Listen, Petrov," Stanton tried again. "We're not in Moscow or the Caucasus. We're on Mars. Even if there might be ghosts on Earth, there aren't any on Mars. Like Oksana said, whatever you think you saw, I'm sure there is some other explanation."

Petrov shook his head. "I do not believe so, Captain. Out of the corner of my eye, I saw a ripple across the control glass. When I looked I saw a figure hurrying through the entry bay. At the same time, there came a rush of cold air. The figure vanished and the cold air left with it."

"That could have been anything," Stanton tried, although he wasn't sure what. "Maybe the reflection of someone in the control glass?"

"Who, Captain?" Petrov asked. "Not Oksana, she was in the comm center. Not Dekker, he was at the roof access. And not you, Mtumbe, Lin or Gold, you were all outside."

Stanton didn't have an answer ready for that.

"And I heard what happened to Agent Gold over the comm link," Petrov added.

"What are you talking about?" Stanton frowned.

"Come now, Captain, you noticed it as well," Petrov answered. "Gold was not, how you say, she was not herself. But if she was not herself, the question is: who was she?"

"You are scaring me, Aleksandr," said Rusakova. "Tell me you do not seriously believe this."

"But I do, Oksana," Petrov replied. "In my village, sometimes people would act strangely. They would say and do things they would never normally do. Afterwards they would not remember everything. It was as if they were in a dream."

"Sounds like they were drunk," Stanton tried to joke.

"On that Russian vodka."

Petrov surrendered a laugh. "Yes, Captain, you are right. It sounds the same. But tell me, was Agent Gold drunk on Russian vodka just now?"

Stanton shrugged. "She's not really an astronaut," he offered, regretting it slightly since he knew Gold was likely listening in through her own comm link. "She probably just got overwhelmed by the strangeness and beauty of it all."

Petrov grinned. "No, Captain, she was overwhelmed, but by a spirit. Some malicious spirit who wishes us all ill."

That was enough for Stanton. The last thing he needed was a ghost scare on top of their already difficult task. "Now you're just talking crazy, Petrov. What spirits are there that could have possessed Gold?"

Petrov smiled, his teeth shining eerily in the half light. "Where are the colonists?" he pointed out.

Again, Stanton didn't have an answer.

"And don't forget," Petrov raised his finger, "there may have been life on Mars at one time."

"Bacteria," countered Stanton. "Maybe. And that was millions of years ago."

"Captain? Sorry to interrupt." It was Dekker over the comm link.

"It's all right," Stanton answered. "What is it?"

"It's Mtumbe," Dekker said. "Something's wrong?"

"Is he breathing all right?"

"His breathing is fine," advised Dekker, "It's his leg."

"What about his leg?"

Dekker hesitated. "I— I think it's infected."

11

"Infected?" Stanton repeated.

"That's what it looks like, Captain," replied Dekker. "Unless you poured foul-smelling yogurt on the cut before to trolloped off with Gold?"

"Trolloped?" Stanton shook his head. "We'll be right there."

He reached under the control glass and pulled out the ship's first aid kit. They hadn't had the time to check out the station's infirmary yet.

"You coming, Petrov?" Stanton challenged. "You've got a fellow crew member down."

Petrov looked up at Rusakova. "You believe me, don't you, Oksana?"

Rusakova smiled softly. "I do believe you, Aleksandr. But I also believe that we have a friend who has been injured. You should come with us so we can help him."

Petrov nodded. "Yes, you are right." He smiled. "I am glad you believe me."

Petrov stood up and headed for the ship's exit. As he reached Stanton, he said, "You still do not believe me, do you,

Captain?"

Stanton was too tired to pretend any more. "No, Petrov, I'm afraid I don't."

Petrov smiled, his grin still unsettling even in the fuller light by the airlock. "That is because you didn't see what Dekker saw."

12

When Stanton and the Russians reached the west airlock, Mtumbe was laying on the floor, sweating profusely, and rolling back and forth in obvious pain. Lin was holding a damp cloth to his head and Dekker was holding a towel against his leg.

"Status report," ordered Stanton.

Dekker lifted the towel. "Look at this."

An oozing pile of white-yellow pus was running out of the gash in Mtumbe's leg.

"Holy shit," Stanton couldn't help but say. "If that's what's coming out—"

"Then what is going into his bloodstream?" finished Lin. "Yes, we thought that as well."

Stanton popped open the first aid kit and pulled out their various forms of antibiotics: spray, injector, and pills. He sprayed the wound first. Mtumbe shrieked and tried to yank his dripping leg away from them. But the spray did its job; the pus practically melted off Mtumbe's leg before evaporating into the air.

Next Stanton shot the injector into Mtumbe's leg, just

above the knee, into the artery. This time Mtumbe only flinched. The extreme pain from the wound site seemed to be dissipating.

But when Stanton tried to give Mtumbe the antibiotic pills, Mtumbe wouldn't open his mouth. He rolled his head side to side, still delusional.

"A little help, gentleman?" Stanton looked up at Dekker and Petrov.

Dekker laid a hold of Mtumbe's head and Petrov forced open his mouth. Stanton pressed the pill down his friend's throat.

"Okay. Let's get him to sick bay," Stanton directed.

Dekker and Petrov lifted him and carried him down the hallway to the station's small infirmary. They placed him on one of the two metal examining tables, then Stanton set the bottle of pills on the counter and started checking the cabinets.

"We'll need more antibiotics," he stated, "Help me find them."

Everyone joined in the search, expect for Lin who was pressing a damp cloth against Mtumbe's head, and Petrov who had started to look until Gold walked next to him. He stared at her, slack-jawed, and backed into a corner. Gold rolled her eyes but kept looking. Stanton decided not to comment—for now. Four people searching for the antibiotics would be enough.

But after a few fruitless minutes, Stanton had to ask, "Any luck?"

"I cannot find any antibiotics at all," Rusakova reported.

"Me neither," said Dekker.

Gold just looked at Stanton and shook her head.

"They were part of their supplies, yes?" asked Lin.

"Of course," answered Stanton. "Enough for seven crew members for eighteen months. They didn't really expect to encounter disease like on Earth, but they weren't about to ignore the possibility either."

"So where are the antibiotics now?" Lin asked.

Stanton put his hands on his hips and stared into the cabinet. "Good question."

"Perhaps they used them all up?" Petrov suggested from his corner, still with that disturbing grin. "It might explain much."

"Hush, Aleksandr," chided Rusakova. "Sometimes you say too much."

Before Petrov could reply, Stanton jumped in. "We all say too much sometimes. Especially at the end of a long, stressful day." He looked at his watch. "Mars's rotation is twenty-three hours and we've had six months on a ship with a twenty-three-hour clock to get used to it. It's time for lights out. God knows we could all use the rest."

Most of the crew nodded, even Gold.

"Gold, show everyone where the crew's quarters are," Stanton instructed. "Someone needs to stay with Commander Mtumbe until he's feeling better. I'll take the first shift, two hours. Who wants the second shift?"

Lin was quick to offer, "I will."

"I'll do the third shift," Dekker said. "No joke."

"Rusakova, can you do fourth shift?" Stanton asked. He didn't trust Petrov's stability yet. If anyone needed a full night's rest, it was Petrov.

And Stanton wanted Gold to sleep through the night as well.

"Yes, Captain," Rusakova answered. "Of course."

"Great," said Stanton. "Everyone just pick a cabin for tonight. It doesn't matter which. We don't know how much longer we'll be here, so no need to select the perfect room. Just a place to sleep tonight."

"I would rather sleep on the ship," Petrov protested.

"Noted," Stanton nodded. "But until we straighten some things out, I want us all to stay together. Mtumbe has to stay in the station, so we all stay in the station."

Petrov shifted his weight and glanced around, but he didn't argue any more.

"You can follow me," Gold said and she headed out of the infirmary toward the sleeping quarters. As they filed out, Stanton heard her say, "I get the first room."

Once everyone was gone, Stanton walked over to Mtumbe and placed a hand on his sweaty arm. He turned off his comm link.

"Don't worry, my friend. I'll get you out of this." Then he lowered his voice. "Once everyone's asleep, I'll head onto the ship and comm back to Earth."

But he could hear Ferguson's scornful voice.

I knew you couldn't do it yourself, Junior. Real leaders don't have friends, they have followers. That's why you'll always be second best.

13

In the event, Stanton couldn't bring himself to leave Mtumbe's side. Mtumbe was sleeping, fitfully at first, then more comfortably. Stanton considered the day. He'd expected something bad, but not any of what had happened. His expectation had been some catastrophic system fail, maybe with the air system, and seven colonist bodies scattered across the station. He wondered whether they would decompose without Earthborne bacteria. Such were his thoughts on the long journey to Mars. The rescue captain expected to be a recovery captain.

But it had turned out to be almost the exact opposite. No colonists' remains to recover, but he had to figure out how to rescue his friend from some virulent Martian bacteria. And he still had his official charge of determining what had happened to the first group.

I don't know what happened to you, Ferguson, he thought, *but being the clean up crew is no picnic either.*

Mercifully his tortured thoughts were interrupted by Lin's arrival. She seemed eager to relieve him. Stanton wondered about the intensity of Lin's feelings for Mtumbe, but he was glad for it under the circumstances. He decided to leave it alone, at least for now. Romantic relationships on this type of a mission could only be a liability. He was still irked that Dekker and Rusakova had hooked up early in the training. But that had only been one night, and they both agreed not to pursue it further.

Gold's face flashed through his mind and he shook his head to clear it.

He was tired, physically and mentally. He needed some sleep. He thanked Lin, who dutifully took her station next to Mtumbe's head, and exited the sick bay, ostensibly for the sleeping quarters.

But he turned toward the entry bay. Time to report to Earth. To hell with Gold's 'exclusive jurisdiction.' There was no sign of the colonists and he had a man down. Although he was loathe to do it, he was pretty sure it was time to request permission to return home.

He was glad the sleeping quarters were about as far away as they could be, and that the crew—that is, Gold—had had a couple hours to fall into a true sleep. The airlock to the ship wasn't all that loud, but it wasn't silent either.

He slid his hands across the control glass and the first set of doors opened for him. A few moments later, the second doors opened and he stepped aboard the *Antares*.

Agent Gold spun around in the pilot's chair.

"Why, Captain Stanton," she grinned. "Fancy meeting you here."

14

"Gold? What are you doing here? I thought I told everyone to get some sleep."

Stanton was flustered but trying not to show it.

"I don't sleep well," Gold replied with a phony shrug. "Why did you come on board? You weren't thinking about radioing back to Earth while I slept, were you?"

"No," Stanton lied, although he questioned why he needed to lie; he was the captain after all. "I just— I thought there might be more medical supplies for Mtumbe."

"Oh good," Gold answered. "I thought with Daniel injured and no sign of the crew, you might be tempted to radio back. Actually that's why I'm here."

"To stop me if I tried?" Stanton demanded. It was one thing to have veto authority over sensitive communications, it was quite another to guard the communications center from him like a guard dog.

"No, silly," Gold laughed. "Guilty conscious, Captain?"

Stanton narrowed his eyes. "No, Gold. I could ask you the same question. If you're not playing Doberman to the comm center, then why are you here?"

"I thought I just told you," Gold answered sweetly. "That's why I'm here. I just commed back to Earth. Let them know we'd arrived and the oxygen levels are acceptable. I also let them know there's a problem with the station's comm equipment."

"Problem?" Stanton repeated. "It's missing."

"Well, I'd say that's a problem, wouldn't you?" she laughed.

"Did you tell them about the colonists or Mtumbe?"

Gold smiled. "Now, see, that's why I'm here. I let them know we were still trying to determine what had happened to the first crew, and I advised them that one of ours had fallen and injured his leg, but was recovering."

"Sounds a little short on details," Stanton observed.

"This is where you figure out I can help you too," Gold said. "It's not just about protecting them from dangerous information from Mars. It's also about protecting us."

Stanton cocked his head to the side. "I'm not following you."

"I told them one of our crew had fallen and hurt his leg. Big deal. Yawn."

"I think it's a big deal," Stanton said.

"I know you do," Gold answered, "and that's why you would have screwed it up."

"Excuse me?" Stanton crossed his arms.

"You would have told them the whole story, wouldn't you have?" Gold accused. "The missing crew? Mtumbe's infection? The missing antibiotics?"

"I— I'm not sure," Stanton stammered. "Maybe."

"And you would have used it to request permission to terminate the mission and return home, right?"

"I don't know," Stanton lied again.

"Do you know what they're reply would have been?"

"I assume it would have been 'Yes,'" Stanton answered.

"It would have been 'Hell no.'"

Stanton was taken aback. "How do you know that?"

"Let me repeat back what you would have said," Gold offered, "but in the way they would have heard it. The colonists are all dead from a mysterious Martian bacteria that all the antibiotics they had couldn't stop. Now one of our crew has been infected. Can we come back and unleash the fatal and incurable epidemic on the people of Earth ensuring the destruction of the human race?"

Stanton's face went ashen.

"Or," Gold finished, "are you going to make us die out here for the sake of all humanity?"

Stanton thought about it for several moments. Finally, he nodded begrudgingly. "I see your point," he admitted.

Gold got up and walked over to Stanton. "You're a good captain. And a good friend to Daniel." She put a hand on his, sending his heart racing. "You want to save Daniel, but you won't do it asking for help. We'll have to do it ourselves."

Stanton wasn't so stupid not to realize she was manipulating him, but his head was spinning with the idea that they wouldn't be allowed to go home.

"I'm done here," Gold said. "Let's head back to the sleeping quarters. You've earned some rest."

Stanton relented and the two of them made their way through the airlock and back to the sleeping wing.

"We saved Captain Ferguson's quarters for you," Gold whispered so as not awaken the others. "We know he was your mentor."

"Something like that," Stanton muttered. Then he whispered, "Thanks. And thanks for sending that message before I sent the wrong one and endangered everyone."

"My pleasure," Gold smiled. "Good night, Captain."

Stanton watched as Gold sauntered to her cabin.

"Good night, Cassie," he whispered.

15

Stanton slept better than he'd expected. He was too tired to stay up worrying about all the things he needed to worry about. He vaguely recalled his dreams had been strange and disturbing, but he couldn't remember them exactly. He was glad for that.

Sitting up in bed, he remembered he was in Ferguson's cabin. He looked around in the daylight. There was almost nothing to show anyone had even used the room. Everything was standard issue, with no personalizations. The only exception was a single photograph taped to the wall opposite the bed. Stanton hadn't noticed it when he'd stumbled into the dark room late last night. But now that it was light, he not only could see it, but he recognized it.

It was the graduation photo from Space Academy, twenty five of the world's top astronauts on the steps of the training facility. His and Ferguson's class. Or maybe he should say Ferguson's and his. Ferguson had graduated top of the class; Stanton had finished second. It would portend their careers as they both moved on from the Academy. Basic training, moon base, asteroid missions, Mars training, and finally Mars Station Alpha. Every step of the way, Ferguson had been the leader and Stanton the assistant. Michael Collins to Ferguson's Neil Armstrong.

Thinking of seconds-in-command reminded Stanton of Mtumbe and roused him from the bed. That's when he noticed Ferguson had written something on top of the photo.

'See you again soon, Junior'

Stanton frowned. He really hated it when Ferguson called him that. A constant reminder of placing second. But it was nice to know Ferguson had been looking forward to seeing him again.

"Too bad it didn't work out," Stanton said aloud as he pulled on his boots to go to breakfast. "Sometimes it's better not to be first, I guess."

The commissary was across the hall from the sleeping cabins. Dekker and Petrov were already there. When Stanton walked in, they stopped talking. Petrov went back to eating his space gruel. Dekker looked up with a huge smile.

"*El Capitan!*" he greeted a bit too loudly. "How did you sleep last night?"

"I slept fine," Stanton answered. "But since you two are both here, I have a question about something Petrov said to me yesterday."

"Oh, don't listen to Petrov," Dekker laughed, tapping his temple. "He's crazy."

Petrov looked at Dekker, but just smiled and kept eating.

Before Stanton could say more, Lin walked in and turned the captain's attention back to more pressing matters. "How's Mtumbe?" he asked.

Lin smiled, "Why don't you ask him yourself?"

Mtumbe limped into the common room with his arms wide and a huge smile on his face.

"Reports of my demise," he laughed, "are greatly exaggerated."

"Daniel!" Stanton rushed over to his friend. "You're okay!"

"Well, I'm on my feet," Mtumbe answered. "I'm not sure I'm okay yet."

He pulled up his pant leg and showed off his gnarled shin. The scar of the original cut was hard to discern among the bumpy, mottled depression surrounding it. It looked like someone had taken a cheese grater and an ice cream scoop to his leg, leaving a six inch long, three inch wide bumpy pink gash in Mtumbe's otherwise smooth brown skin.

"Damn," said Stanton. "That looks like hell."

"Well, I'm done eating!" announced Dekker as he pushed away his cereal.

Mtumbe looked down at his mangled limb. "Yeah, it's pretty nasty. Hell of a souvenir, eh, cap?"

"It's not so bad, Commander," said Lin. "It is a battle scar. You can be proud."

Mtumbe smiled down at her. "Lin stayed the whole night with me. She helped me pull back to the surface."

Stanton cocked his head. "What about Dekker?" Stanton looked over at the Dutchman. "And Rusakova? We had a schedule."

"Lin told me to go back to sleep," Dekker shrugged. "And she outranks me, so I really had no choice."

"I also told Oksana to let me stay with Commander Mtumbe," Lin explained. "He seemed to be responding to me."

Mtumbe nodded.

Stanton didn't like the fact that his orders had been disregarded, and he didn't like that one of his crew had spent the entire night awake. Lin would be exhausted later today whether she was willing to admit it or not. They would have to make accommodations for that, thereby impacting the mission.

But he couldn't argue with the results.

"Thank you, Lieutenant Lin," he said. "We'll get you some rest today."

"You can sleep on the ship," Dekker said. "We're heading home today, right, Captain?"

Stanton smiled at him. "Well, I was thinking about an excursion," he said, "but we're not heading home just yet. We haven't completed our mission."

"Why not?" Dekker argued. "We know the colonists didn't survive, and I sure as hell hope you're not planning on keeping us here eighteen months. I think you'd have a mutiny on your hands."

The last sentence was a joke, but mutiny wasn't anything to joke about. Even Petrov winced at the word. Dekker blushed.

"What I mean, is—" he tried to explain.

"I know what you meant, Lieutenant," Stanton interrupted. "Why don't you stop with the jokes for a bit and finish your breakfast?"

"*Da*," mumbled Petrov through the last of his own food.

"Besides, Dekker," Stanton was happy to say, "I need you to be ready for a surface walk in thirty minutes."

Dekker choked on his gruel. "Wha—? Who, me? Why

me?"

"Well, it ain't gonna be me," said Mtumbe. "I did my turn."

"That's what I'm worried about," said Dekker. "I don't want it to be my turn next. I'm allergic to killer space viruses."

"It was bacteria," corrected Lin. Then she turned to Stanton. "Will I be going on the surface walk, Captain?"

"I was thinking about having you come along," Stanton answered, "but you need your rest."

Lin looked disappointed.

"And I need someone I can trust to watch after Mtumbe," Stanton added. "I'm not convinced he should be up and around just yet."

Lin's look of disappointment melted away. "Yes, sir. Thank you, sir."

"So who is going with us, Captain?" Dekker asked. "I don't trust myself alone with you."

Stanton decided to ignore the joke rather than respond to it. "Petrov and Rusakova," he answered.

Petrov just nodded, apparently nonplussed by the assignment.

"Where is Rusakova?" Stanton asked looking around the small eating room.

"Right here, Captain," said Rusakova as she entered the room with Gold right behind her. "What am I needed for?"

"You, Petrov, Dekker, and I are going on a surface walk," explained Stanton.

"Why?" demanded Gold.

"Don't worry," said Dekker. "You're not coming. It's my turn to die from a horrible Martian bacterial infection."

Mtumbe threw up his arms. "I'm not dead," he

reminded everyone.

Gold turned to Stanton. "No, seriously. What's the purpose of the walk?"

Once again Gold was challenging his authority in front of the rest of the crew. This time it wasn't even on a communications issue. Stanton was starting to believe she didn't even know when she was doing it.

"It's right up your alley, Agent Gold," Stanton answered. "We're going to find that comm equipment."

Everyone just stared at Stanton for several seconds.

Finally Gold asked, "And where do you think it is, buried out back with some dog bones?"

Stanton forced a laugh. "No, no, of course not." He walked over to Dekker and placed his hands on the Dutchman's shoulders. "Nils here saw something when we were flying in for our landing."

Dekker looked at Petrov. "'Nils'?"

Petrov just shrugged and smiled.

"Now that we know the comm equipment has been removed," Stanton went on, "it seems like a good possibility that's what Dekker saw. So we're going to find out."

"Uh, Captain?" Dekker said uneasily, glancing nervously at Petrov, "I don't think—"

"Don't worry, Nils," Stanton interrupted. "I know it was pretty far from here, but we'll use the station's rover."

"Is that even working?" Gold questioned.

"Only one way to find out," Stanton grinned. "So far everything else has been in perfect working order."

When no one else said anything, Stanton announced, "Good. It's agreed. Thirty minutes, meet at the entry bay to suit up. I'm going to clean up and grab something to eat."

Gold stared at Dekker as he stood up to go get ready for the excursion.

"Don't stare at me so long, Agent," he said as he walked past her. "People will talk."

Gold offered a half-smile. "They always do, eventually."

16

"Captain? Do you have a moment?"

Dekker had followed Stanton to the bathroom.

"Um, I'm kinda busy just now, Dekker," he answered from inside one of the small toilet closets.

"I know," said Dekker, "but this may the only chance to speak privately with you."

Stanton flushed the toilet and stepped out. "I was almost done anyway." Then he stepped over to sterilize his hands with the septic lotion. "I thought you might follow me."

Dekker nodded and shrugged. "What I saw," he got right to it. "It wasn't comm equipment."

"I know," Stanton smiled.

"You know?"

"Well, I figured," Stanton turned around as he rubbed his hands together. "I know you saw something, and based on what Petrov said, I figured it wasn't abandoned comm equipment."

"What did Petrov tell you?"

"He told me that if I had seen what you saw, then I'd

believe there could be ghosts on Mars."

Dekker's face went ashen. "I— I'm not sure about that exactly."

"Dekker," Stanton put a hand on his shoulder. "Nils. Why don't you just tell me what you saw?"

But before he could, Gold walked in. It was a unisex facility. They were all professionals.

"Captain, can I have a word?" she asked.

Dekker gladly pulled away from his captain. "See you the entry bay," he grinned. "Enjoyed discussing urination styles with you. Ta ta!"

And he hurried out as fast as he could.

Gold watched him leave, then turned to Stanton. "He's an idiot."

"Maybe," Stanton agreed, "but he's our idiot. So what did you want to talk to me about?"

"What's the reason for this excursion?" Gold asked.

"I thought you were there when I said—"

"No, the real reason," Gold interrupted. "There's no way the comm equipment is sitting outside over the nearest ridge."

"Well, for one thing," Stanton said, "it's not the nearest ridge. It's like three or four ridges away. For another, that comm equipment is somewhere, and it doesn't appear to be anywhere inside the station, so it must be out there. Plus, it's not like you can burn anything in that CO2 atmosphere, so if it is there, it's probably still in one piece."

Gold crossed her arms.

"Look, Dekker saw something," Stanton went on. "You heard him as we were getting ready to land. It might be the comm equipment. If not, maybe it's something else that will help us solve the mystery of the missing colonists."

Gold frowned. "I don't believe you," she said simply. "You're not telling me everything. I thought you trusted me."

Stanton wasn't sure why she thought that all of a sudden, but he felt bad nevertheless. "Look, I'm telling you the truth. Dekker saw something. It may help us figure this all out. That's all."

"That's all?"

"That's all." Stanton smiled broadly. He hoped she bought it.

"Okay," Gold said finally. "I'll man the comm center to act as your home base and monitor your communications."

"M— Monitor our communications?" Stanton choked. "I don't— That is, well." Then he tried smiling in a way he hoped was charming. "I thought you trusted me."

Gold laughed. "No, Captain. I don't trust you at all."

Stanton didn't know what to say. So Gold spoke again.

"You'd better hurry and get into your suit," she teased. "You don't want to be late for your own excursion."

17

By the time Stanton got to the entry bay, Petrov and Rusakova were already suited up and Dekker was trying to select which suit to use. He picked one and held it up in front of himself.

"Does this make me look fat?"

"Oh my God, shut up, Dekker," said Mtumbe. The entire crew had traveled down to the entry bay. Mtumbe was sitting on a small stool next to the control panel. His leg was mostly covered by his pants, but the gnarled scar stuck down below the cuff.

Stanton walked up to Dekker. "Just pick a suit already. They're all the same."

When Dekker hesitated, Stanton took the orange spacesuit from him. "I'll wear this one. You grab another one. Last one dressed has to clean Mtumbe's wound."

Dekker looked expressionlessly at the captain. "That's not funny," he said.

"Not very sensitive either," complained Mtumbe. "I'm right here."

"Just pick a suit, Dekker," Stanton sighed. "We need to get a move on."

"Well, I really liked that one," Dekker pointed to the one Stanton had taken, "but I'll just have to make do with another."

He turned around and grabbed the suit nearest him. "I hate buying off the rack," he huffed importantly.

Stanton turned his attention to suiting up and within a few minutes, Lin and Mtumbe were checking everyone's seals. Gold had walked in too, but was leaning against the wall by the door.

Once the helmets were secure, Stanton tested the comm link. "Test, one, two, three. Rusakova, do you copy?"

"Roger," answered Rusakova.

"Petrov, do you copy?"

"*Da.*"

"Dekker, do you copy?"

"No, but I do wash windows and iron. I'll make someone a wonderful wife."

Stanton grimaced. "Careful, Nils, or we'll leave you out there."

Dekker thought for a moment, and smiled. "Roger that."

"I'll monitor communications," Gold announced from her hiding spot by the door.

"Monitor communications?" Mtumbe asked. "For what?"

"For trouble," Gold answered. "Like what happened on the roof walk."

"You mean like what you caused on the roof walk?" Mtumbe growled.

Gold's face started to flush and she looked to Stanton, but he just raised an eyebrow behind his helmet's face shield. Gold sighed.

"Yes," she said. "Like I caused. I'm sorry about that. I don't know what happened to me out there."

"I do," whispered Petrov, but it was picked up by the comm link and was broadcast to the others' helmets.

Stanton didn't visibly react, but he continued to straighten out and double check his suit while he whispered back, "Hush, Petrov."

Mtumbe stared at Gold for a minute, then that smile of his flashed onto his face. "Apology accepted," he said. "It can be overwhelming the first time you set out for a spacewalk. Or a Marswalk, I guess."

Gold offered the smallest of smiles back. "Thank you, Commander. I'm sure that's all it was."

"No it wasn't," sang Petrov to his spacesuited crew mates.

"Shut up, Petrov," Stanton sang back.

Then Stanton pointed at the comm icon on the entry bay command glass. Lin saw the gesture and pressed the icon to connect the spacesuits' comm links with the station's comm center. One more icon and Stanton and the rest could be heard through the glass.

"Once Dekker finally gets his suit on—"

"I'm good!" shouted the Dutchman, suited arms spread wide to show everyone.

"Okay, then," Stanton said, "Now that Dekker finally has his suit on, we're ready to go. We'll go through the south airlock to the station's rover. If everything is in order, we'll head out to whatever it was Dekker saw. We'll have our comm links on at all times so you can monitor for emergencies."

Gold, Mtumbe, and Lin all nodded.

"Gold will monitor communications," Stanton went on, "and Lin will station herself at the airlock in case we need quick access back into the station."

Mtumbe shrugged. "What about me?"

Stanton smiled. "You get some rest," he said. "And that's an order. You were practically dead yesterday."

Mtumbe started to protest, but Stanton interrupted, "I said it was an order."

Stanton knew that would be enough to sway his recalcitrant, but dutiful, second-in-command.

"Aye aye, Captain." Mtumbe shrugged again. "I'll be in my cabin if anyone needs me." Then he thought for a moment. "Which one's my cabin? I spent last night in the sick bay."

"It's the one next to mine," Lin said, with the smallest of smiles.

Mtumbe nodded and headed off. Then he stopped again. "Which one is your cabin?"

"They all look very similar," Lin agreed. "You will know it because I placed my Quan Yin statue in there. Your cabin is to the right of mine."

Mtumbe gave a smile and a thumbs up. "Quan Yin. Got it."

Then he turned to Stanton and the out-crew. "Good luck, guys."

"Get some rest," Stanton ordered again. Then he activated the airlock to the equipment bay. He watched through the glass as first Mtumbe then Gold headed back into the station.

He waited until he thought she was in the comm center

then began yelling, "Gold?! Gold?! Where the hell are you?"

18

"I— I'm right here, Captain!" Gold yelled as she turned on the comm feed. "Sorry, I was just talking to Commander Mtumbe and—"

"Never mind that, we need help," barked Stanton.

"What's the situation? Is a man down? Do you need a rescue team? Should I send Lin out to get you?"

Dekker started laughing.

"No, no," said Stanton. "It's not an emergency. We just need you to open the outer equipment bay door from the control room. The rover's operational, but all exterior entry pads seem to have been disabled. We can't get the doors to open and I don't want to come back through the airlock if we don't have to."

"Well, I guess that explains why the key panel wouldn't let us back in yesterday from the roof walk," Gold observed.

"Neh, poltergeist," murmured Petrov.

"What did he say?" Gold asked.

"Nothing," said Stanton. "Shut up, Petrov," he ordered.

"Did he say poltergeist?" Gold followed up.

"No," said Stanton.

"Yes," said Petrov.

"Shut. Up. Petrov," repeated Stanton.

"The lady asked a question," Petrov defended.

"Can you just open the bay doors please, Agent?"

"Why does Petrov think we have a poltergeist?" Gold asked.

"Because I saw it, dear lady," said Petrov over the comm link. "And because poltergeists like to sabotage things."

"No more, Petrov," said Stanton. "That's an order."

"He may have a point," Gold said, trying to sound casual. Stanton knew she was fishing for information. "The explosion, the word carved in the wall, the comm equipment, my stumble on the ladder, and now the entry pads. A poltergeist would explain all that."

"She is a smart woman, Captain," Petrov said with a chuckle. "You should listen to her more."

"Thank you, Aleksandr," said Gold over the comm link. "I do feel better knowing I may have been pushed down that ladder."

"I believe it was likely something far more sinister, Agent Gold," warned Petrov.

"More sinister?" she asked.

"Okay, we're done," announced Stanton. "No more of this talk. We have a mission to complete. You two can talk ghost stories after dinner tonight. Just open the door."

"Come now, Captain," Gold protested, "I was just—"

"Open the God damn door, Gold," barked Stanton. "Now! That's an order."

Gold was silent for a moment. "Captain?"

"That's an order," growled Stanton. "Can you ever just follow a damned order, Agent?"

Gold was quiet for a moment. Then she said simply, "Yes, sir."

The equipment bay doors buzzed and began to swing open. Following Stanton's outburst, everyone was quiet. They all climbed silently into the rover and Stanton drove out onto the Martian landscape.

"Captain?" Gold said over the comm feed once they had cleared the station.

Stanton hesitated, then responded, "Yes, Agent Gold?"

"Given the information just conveyed," she announced, "and my concerns for the stability of the person who conveyed it, I am hereby terminating all communication with Earth, except through me."

She waited a moment, then added, "That's also an order."

The others looked at Stanton, even as they bounced over the red rocks. But Stanton stared straight ahead as he drove the rover.

"We'll see who's in charge of communications, Agent," Stanton said. Then he reached up and turned off his comm link's distant feed back to the station.

Petrov smiled and followed suit. Dekker did too. Rusakova hesitated, then turned hers off as well. They could now speak to each other, but their transmissions would not relay back to the station.

"I am not sure this is a good idea," worried Rusakova. "Decisions made in anger are seldom wise."

"Anger, my dear Oksana?" Petrov laughed as Stanton

smiled broadly. "There is no anger. That went exactly as planned."

19

"What do you mean?" Rusakova asked as the rover continued its trek across the Martian landscape.

They were headed east from the station, toward a small valley beyond a rise. Mars Station Alpha was built on the edge of the Amazonis Plains, one of the largest and smoothest plateaus on the planet. Geological evidence confirmed water once flowed on Mars and this was likely the southern shore of Mars' vast northern ocean. Sitting in the shadow of Olympus Mons, the station was essentially beachfront property for an ocean that had disappeared a billion years earlier.

As a result, while the land immediately surrounding the station was exceptionally smooth, it soon gave way to the hills and ridges more commonly associated with terrestrial landscape. The rover was a six-wheeled, solar powered device, designed specifically for this kind of mission: exploring a place too far to reach safely on foot.

Stanton found the expanse of the landscape a bit disorienting. Although there were ridges and hills and rocks, everything was the same rusty orange color, even the towering mountain Olympus Mons that dominated the horizon. So although they knew where they were headed roughly, the landscape seemed to offer no other landmarks for guidance.

"Do you mean you tried to get Gold mad at you?" Rusakova asked again.

"I wanted to be able to talk with the three of you in confidence," Stanton explained. "Agent Gold insisted on monitoring our communications. If I had refused, she would have been suspicious. Similarly, if we had just turned off our comm feed for no reason, she would have known that we didn't want her to hear us. As it is now, she thinks we turned them off out of anger."

"I was not trying to make her angry," Petrov said. "I was just telling her what I have seen."

Stanton looked over at the cosmonaut. "Please don't start again, Petrov. I was going to get angry about opening the equipment bay doors, but the ghost thing was way better. Still, that doesn't mean I want to hear more about Russian ghost legends."

"All of this trickery is very confusing," Rusakova said. "Why are we really out here?"

Dekker answered that one. "He wants to see what I saw."

"And what did you see?" asked Rusakova.

Dekker raised his hand and pointed ahead as they crested a large ridge.

"That."

20

Ahead of them was the red palette version of Salisbury Plain.

Large rectangular stones, some over three meters tall, were tipped upright, arranged in an irregular semicircle. There were seven total: the tallest in the middle, with three on each side of descending height. The smallest end stone was less than two meters tall. In the middle of the semicircle was another stone laying flat, partially covered in the Martian sand that constantly blew through the thin carbon dioxide atmosphere.

Stanton parked the rover and they approached the monument on foot. All the stones were worn and rounded. They looked ancient.

"Oh, my dear God," Petrov gasped over the comm link. "There are ghosts here. There was life here. And their ghosts stalk us now!"

"Calm down, Aleksandr," Rusakova said, patting his shoulder. "There is likely some other explanation for this." She paused. "Although I'm not sure what it is."

"So this is what you saw, Dekker?" Stanton asked. He was focusing on the mundane process of how they came to find it because he didn't want to contemplate the enormity of the significance of the site itself.

Dekker nodded for several moments before finally answering, "Yes, Captain. I wasn't exactly sure what I saw from above as we flew in. It looked architectural to me somehow. But now that we're standing here, there is no doubt. This is what I saw."

Rusakova frowned. "Why have we not seen this before?" she demanded. "Satellites have mapped every square centimeter of Mars. Surely this would have been seen."

Stanton thought of Gold suddenly being added to their mission.

"Just because the people at the top see something," he said, "doesn't mean they let anyone else see it. People have been claiming they've seen structures in Martian satellite photos since the days of the original Viking explorers almost a century ago. Maybe our higher-ups know all about this, but just never told us."

"That's a pretty sick joke," Dekker said.

"Do you think the first crew found this too?" Rusakova asked.

"Maybe," contemplated Stanton.

"Maybe they reported back but Command squashed the information," Dekker suggested. "In fact, maybe they didn't really disappear when Mars went behind the sun. Maybe they sent communications but Command hid them from the world. Maybe Command made sure they never made it back to Earth to tell the truth!"

"Command had nothing to do with the colonists

disappearing," Stanton shot back, although he wasn't completely convinced of his words. "We don't know yet what happened to them, but I will not brook suggestions that our Command intentionally sabotaged the mission, and sacrificed the lives of those colonists, just because some information about a Martian Stonehenge might be hard for some of the public to swallow."

"It does explain Agent Gold's presence," Rusakova observed.

Stanton had no reply.

"Maybe Command did nothing to the colonists," Petrov offered. "Maybe the colonists found this and did something to anger the ghosts who rest here."

"Knock off the crazy talk, Petrov," said Stanton. "This is serious."

"Oh, but I am very serious," responded Petrov. "You said you did not believe in ghosts on Mars because there was never life on Mars. Well, now you know better. Do you still believe there cannot be ghosts here?"

"Even if this was made by Martians," Stanton argued, "that would have been billions of years ago."

"Let me ask you, Captain," said Petrov. "How long do ghosts survive?"

Stanton just stared at Petrov, unsure how to answer him.

Meanwhile, Dekker climbed atop the central stone and raised his arms over his head. "I am the High Mighty Priest of all of Mars!" he declared. "Woe be to those who sully my shrine!"

"Stop goofing around already, Dekker," said Stanton. "I want to see what we can learn about this place."

"I am the Oracle of Dekker!" He ignored the captain. "Ask me a question, any question, and the spirits of Mars past shall speak their answer through me."

"You should not ridicule spirits," Petrov warned. "There are things we do not understand but which exist nonetheless. Respect them."

But Dekker danced up and down on the rock, waving his arms and mimicking ghost noises, "Oo-ooh!"

"Ignore him for now, I guess," said Stanton. "Let's go take a look at that first stone there."

Stanton turned toward the ruddy stone when Dekker suddenly said, "Hey, did anybody else just get really cold?"

"Oh, shit," said Stanton, looking back to his crewman.

Dekker's suit was failing. It wasn't properly inflated any more. Instead, it hung loosely like a jacket and slacks.

"Aw, crap," Dekker said as he started coughing against the carbon dioxide seeping into his spacesuit. "I knew I shouldn't have bought off the rack."

21

Stanton ran over to Dekker and turned his air valve all the way open, just as he'd done for Mtumbe.

"Hang on, Dekker!" he shouted. "We'll get you back to station in time."

Dekker coughed and smiled weakly, but it wasn't working as well as it had with Mtumbe. Mtumbe had had a single tear in his suit at the bottom of a pant leg. Dekker's suit was suffering from multiple points of failure. Carbon dioxide was seeping in at every crevice, including right where his helmet connected to the suit.

Stanton and Petrov picked up Dekker, one on each side, and hurried back to the rover. Rusakova ran ahead and jumped in the driver's seat. As soon as the three men had piled in, she pressed the accelerator and peeled out in the Martian sand.

The rover raced across the rocks and bumps, far too fast, while Stanton implored Dekker to, "Hold on. Just hold on."

Dekker started coughing heavily, then gasping as the

station came into sight. Rusakova tried to make the rover go faster, but the throttle was already all the way open.

Stanton turned his comm feed back on. "Gold! Gold! Come in, Gold!"

"Oh, there you are," came Gold's cold, snarky tone. "Decided to talk to me after all—"

"Shut up, Gold!" Stanton barked. "Open the equipment bay doors!"

"You can stop yelling at me now, Captain," Gold said. "I'm just—"

"Man down!" Stanton interrupted. "Dekker's suit failed. Open the damn doors!"

Gold was silent for a moment, then replied simply, "Yes, Captain."

Stanton could see the equipment bay doors start to swing open as they approached.

"Oh, Nils," Rusakova whispered through tears. "Please do not die."

"Lin?" Stanton said into the comm link.

"I'm at the airlock, Captain," she replied. "The outer airlock door is already open for you."

Rusakova drove the rover into the bay so fast she couldn't stop it in time and it crashed to a stop into the back wall. Stanton and Petrov jumped off and pulled Dekker from the rover. They ran into the airlock with Rusakova right behind. As soon as they were inside, Lin closed the airlock door behind them and flooded the chamber with the oxygen-rich air of the station.

Stanton disconnected Dekker's helmet and pulled it off. Dekker was completely unresponsive. His eyes bulged slightly and his tongue protruded from his mouth.

"Nils!" shouted Rusakova. She tried to reach him, but Petrov held her back and she collapsed into his arms.

Lin rushed in with the ventrofibrillator and applied it to Dekker, shoving the mouthpiece past his swollen tongue all the way back into his airway.

Lin activated it once. Twice. Three times.

Each time, Dekker's body convulsed, but his breathing never started again.

Gold ran into the airlock, followed by Mtumbe with a limping run, but neither said anything.

Lin looked at Stanton who looked back at her with gaunt eyes.

She activated the ventrofibrillator a fourth time. A fifth time. A sixth time. Nothing.

Lin shook her head. "I'm sorry, Captain."

Oksana Rusakova broke away from Petrov and dropped to her knees. She hugged her one time lover's body and sobbed, "Nils! No!"

But for naught. Dekker was dead.

22

"What the hell happened out there?!" demanded Gold.

Stanton pulled off his helmet and swallowed against the lump in his throat. "His suit failed."

Petrov looked gravely at the captain, but then at Oksana sobbing atop Dekker body, and said nothing.

"Failed?" Gold repeated. "What does that mean, failed?"

"It means his suit failed," Stanton growled. "The seams failed and carbon dioxide flooded the suit."

"Why didn't you turn up the air flow like with Mtumbe?" Gold accused.

"I did, Gold," Stanton defended. "This was a different situation. Dekker suit wasn't just breeched, it failed completely. The air flow, even at its highest, couldn't ward off the CO_2 coming in right at his neck. Plus we were a lot farther away."

Gold's voice shot up. "And why was that, Captain? What was so important out there? And why did you have to shut off the comm feed?"

"Yes!" shouted Rusakova, still hugging Dekker's lifeless body. "Why did we have to go on that fool's errand and turn off our comm feed? It endangered all of us and now Nils is dead!"

"The comm feed wouldn't have saved him," Stanton answered.

"And it was important what we saw," said Petrov.

Gold looked back and forth between Stanton and Petrov. "What did you see?" she demanded.

"Yes, Captain, tell them!" shrieked Rusakova. "Tell them what idiocy cost Nils his life!"

"Okay, now is not the time for this," Stanton said. "We have a man down and we need to make arrangements."

He pulled himself upright. "Mtumbe, take Rusakova to her cabin to rest. Stay with her and get her anything she needs."

"Yes, Captain," Mtumbe said. He offered a hand to Rusakova. "Come on, Oksana. There's nothing more to do right now."

Rusakova took Mtumbe's hand and stood up. She wiped the tears from her face and looked right at the captain. "Do not dispose of his body until I can say goodbye."

"Of course not," assured Stanton. "He will receive a proper burial."

Mtumbe put his arm around Rusakova's shoulder and guided the crying cosmonaut out of the airlock and toward the sleeping quarters.

Stanton placed a hand on Petrov's shoulder. "Can you and Lin take Dekker to sick bay? We'll need to remove the suit for a full inspection."

"Yes, Captain," replied Petrov gravely. "This is bad. It

will only get worse now."

Stanton grabbed Petrov by both shoulders. "I need you here, Aleksandr, not on the family farm in Novogorod. Do this for me now. We'll talk about the rest later."

Petrov nodded. "Yes, Captain." But he didn't look good. His face was even more gaunt and his eyes were like dull rocks pushed into his skull.

Petrov lifted Dekker's body under the arms and Lin picked up the feet, then they carried it out of the airlock.

Stanton led Gold out of the airlock as well and closed the interior door behind them.

"Now," he said sitting down on a chair. "You and I need to talk."

23

"We don't need to talk," spat Gold. "You need to explain. What the hell is wrong with you? Why did you turn off your comm feed?"

Stanton hesitated. He wanted to tell her, but he didn't totally trust her. Or maybe that wasn't it. Maybe he was starting to think Petrov might be right and he was ashamed and embarrassed to admit it.

"Do you remember what Petrov said?" he asked.

Gold stared at him for a moment, trying to sort through all the things that all the different crew had told her since they'd arrived. "You'll have to be more specific, Captain."

There was something in the way she said 'captain' that suggested she didn't really respect the title.

Stanton shifted uneasily on his stool. "About—" He couldn't believe he was saying it. "About the poltergeist?"

If Stanton had ever wondered what it felt like to have someone look at him like he was crazy, he didn't need to wonder any longer. Gold's eyes flew open wide and she took a step back.

"Are you fucking kidding me?" she said. "A poltergeist? You think the station is haunted by a poltergeist?"

Stanton stood up and put out his hands. "No, no, that's not what I mean. It's—"

He didn't know where to start. "Do you remember how Petrov screamed and abandoned his post when we were on the roof?"

"Yes," Gold replied warily.

"And do you remember how Dekker said he saw something when we were flying in for the landing at the station?"

Again, Gold offered a wary, "Yes."

"Okay," Stanton exhaled. "I told you we were going to look for the missing comm equipment."

"Yes, you did," answered Gold. "Was that even true?"

Stanton smiled and shrugged. "Not exactly, no."

Gold crossed her arms. "I don't appreciate being lied to, Captain."

Stanton nodded. "Understood. But what I'm trying to say is—"

"Captain!" Mtumbe rushed into the room, still limping.

"What is it?" Stanton asked.

Mtumbe looked at Gold, and frowned. "Um, it's, uh..."

"Oh, for God's sake!" Gold threw her hands up. "I'll leave. You weren't making any sense anyway, Captain. I'll go see if Petrov and Lin need any help."

As she walked away, she muttered, "I bet Petrov will tell me what really happened."

Mtumbe and Stanton watched Gold leave, then Stanton opined, "She's a problem."

"Agreed," said Mtumbe, "but we may have a bigger one."

24

"What?" asked Stanton.

"Oksana told me what you found out there," Mtumbe started.

Stanton shook his head. "It was amazing, Daniel. I don't even know what to think."

Mtumbe nodded. Then he reached into his pocket and pulled something out. "Look at this," he said as he unfurled his hand from the object.

In his hand was a small figurine, carved from the same rock the monoliths had been made of. It was worn and rounded and looked like little more than a long bumpy rock. But at the same time, the shape of humanoid figure was still visible trapped inside the ancient artifact.

"Where did you find that?" Stanton whispered. Its significance, when combined with the standing stones he'd just seen, didn't escape him.

"It was in Mei-Zhu's room."

"Lin found it?" Stanton asked, not completely understanding.

Mtumbe shook his head. "I don't think so. When I asked which room was mine, she told me it was next to hers and I could tell her room because it had a Quan Yin statue in it. I went to the room I thought was hers and poked around looking for the statue."

"But you found this instead," Stanton finished.

"Actually I found the statue too," Mtumbe answered. "But this was inside the closet, up on the top shelf."

"How much were you snooping around?" Stanton cocked his head at his friend.

Mtumbe flashed that disarming smile. "Hot chick tells you you can snoop around her bedroom? C'mon, man, that's prime intelligence gathering."

Stanton nodded. "There must be something in the air," he mumbled. Then, troubled by the thought, he changed the subject back. "So what is it?"

Mtumbe looked at him. "Are you kidding?"

Stanton looked at the ancient figurine. It was getting hard to deny what the evidence was showing them. Ancient figurines and standing stones. Man had always wondered if there had been life on Mars. Had they just discovered proof? Had Ferguson's crew found it first? And did it have anything to do with their unexplained disappearance?

"Did you tell Lin?" he asked.

"Not yet," Mtumbe answered. "But I was going to."

Stanton nodded again. "Of course, of course." He thought for a moment. "Can you wait a bit to tell her?"

Mtumbe looked sideways at him. "Why?"

"There's a lot of information exploding at us just now," Stanton answered. "And I just can't believe we're the first ones to learn about this. Did Command know about this? And if so, why didn't they tell us?"

Stanton shook his head. "I don't know who to trust."

Mtumbe reached out and put a hand on his friend's shoulder. "Do you trust me?" he asked.

Stanton looked Mtumbe in the eye. "You know I do."

"Then listen to me," Mtumbe said. "It's not good to have secrets."

Just then Gold walked back in. She crossed her arms and glowered at them. "Okay, what are you two whispering about?"

25

Stanton leaned back and smiled. "No whispering here, Agent. Just discussing our situation, and what to do next."

Gold uncrossed her arms and stepped in to join them, albeit warily. "I caught Petrov in the hall. He told me what you found out there."

Stanton nodded. "I figured he would. What else did he say?"

Mtumbe casually slid the figurine back into his pocket. If Gold saw, she didn't make it known.

"He said Dekker defiled the site and was punished by the spirits who dwell there."

Stanton raised an eyebrow. "Did he really?"

"He even said 'dwell'?" Mtumbe asked.

"Oh yes," Gold answered. "I definitely remember the phrase 'spirits who dwell there.' A lot of the rest was rambling, but Lin and I got the basic gist of it."

"Surprised?" Stanton asked.

Gold raised an eyebrow. "Surprised about the structure you found? Well, yes."

"Surprised it's there?" Stanton clarified. "Or surprised we found it?"

"What's that supposed to mean?" Gold hissed.

"You're State Department, not NASA," Stanton said. "How do we know you didn't know about this the whole time? Maybe that's why you're in charge of communications, so we can't tell the world the truth about Mars."

Gold smiled tightly. "So Petrov's not the only paranoid delusional on this crew, I see."

She looked to Mtumbe for support, but he just shrugged. "It's a lot all at once," he said. "Did you know about Mars Henge?"

"Of course not," Gold spat. "I don't know anything about this damned trip. I was working on commercial extradition treaty synchronization when I got plucked and reassigned to this godforsaken, doomed mission. They didn't tell me squat except that my role was 'vital,'" she made air quotes in front of her face, "and that I needed to keep the safety of the crew and the public on Earth in mind at all times."

She frowned. "They did tell me that we might find something that simply couldn't be reported back to Earth for public safety reasons. I assumed they meant something about what happened to the first crew."

"That is probably what they meant," Mtumbe agreed.

Stanton seemed less sure. He recalled Ferguson's advice once regarding their civilian commanders:

We're nothing more than tools to them. They'd be out here if they could, but they can't. They can't because they're weak, and old, and cowardly. But they want power and control. So they send us to do the work, then they decide for themselves how to divvy up the fruits of our labor. And the worst part is, we let them do it, because we don't give a damn about power, we just want to be out here. We need to be out here. It's who we are. We can't change that. So they use us, but never forget: we're the ones who get to see the whole damned planet while we stand with our feet on the fucking moon.

"You like being out here?" Stanton suddenly asked Gold.

She had trouble with the change in conversation. "Where? The entry bay?"

Stanton smiled and shook his head. "No. Space. Mars. Off Earth."

"Oh," said Gold. Then she smiled broadly. "Yeah. I like it a lot."

"What do you like about it?" Stanton continued.

Gold thought for a moment. "It's so new. No one's been here before. Well, almost no one anyway. But we're here and we're seeing what no one ever even used to dream of seeing."

"What if you see something you're not supposed to see?" Stanton pressed.

Gold thought about that one long and hard. She looked at Stanton, then Mtumbe, then the floor, then Stanton again. "I don't think it's possible to see something we're not supposed to see. We're here to see things and whatever we see is what we're supposed to see."

Stanton smiled. "Be careful, Agent. You're sounding like one of us."

Gold laughed. "It was bound to happen eventually. But don't misunderstand me," she warned. "Just because we're meant to see something doesn't mean everyone on Earth needs to hear about it."

Stanton and Mtumbe both frowned.

"Then what's the point of us seeing it?" Mtumbe asked.

"I would think it would be its own reward," Gold chided. "So no, there's no way I'm letting you comm back that you found Mars Henge."

Stanton stood up, ready to challenge her, but just then Lin walked in.

"I removed the spacesuit from Lieutenant Dekker," she announced. "I would suggest we dispose of the body quickly. That Martian bacteria might be on him too. We saw what it did to Daniel's leg."

"Well, Gold," Stanton said to his communications czar. "We at least have to tell them one of crew has died."

Gold's eyes narrowed. "We don't have to tell them anything unless *I* decide we tell them. You and I have already discussed the dangers in Command misinterpreting our communiqués. Let's think this one over before we decide what, if anything, to inform them of at this time."

"Man," Mtumbe slapped his thigh, "you are one cold-blooded bitch."

Somehow, that made Stanton angry, which in turn made him confused. Gold, however, didn't seem phased. "Thanks for noticing, Commander. They didn't select me for this job because of my long blond hair."

Stanton needed to change the subject.

"Where's Petrov?" he asked Lin.

"As soon as we placed the body in the sick bay, he left to check on Commander Rusakova," Lin answered. "If what he said is true, I'm sure she's very upset."

"What did he say?" Stanton asked.

"And did he use the word 'dwell'?" asked Mtumbe.

"I don't recall his exact words, I'm afraid," Lin

answered, "but he said you found an ancient Martian temple and when Dekker jumped on the altar and defiled it, his suit failed. Petrov is convinced the ghosts did it."

"Which ghosts?" Gold sneered. "The Mars Henge spirits or the poltergeist?" Then she stepped toward the doorway. "I'm going to use the little astronaut's room. When I get back, we should discuss how to phrase our communication to Command regarding Dekker's death. I can already tell you we're not using the words 'ancient temple,' 'altar,' or 'ghosts.'"

"What about 'dwell'?" Mtumbe asked with a grin.

Gold grinned back, but without any warmth whatsoever. "Unlikely," she said, "except maybe that now he dwells with angels."

With that, Gold slipped down the hallway.

"That woman is cold," said Mtumbe.

"And a liar," added Lin.

Stanton and Mtumbe both looked at Lin.

"Why do you say that?" Stanton demanded, trying not to sound upset by the accusation.

Lin shrugged casually. "Because it is true. She lied to all of us. She did not carve 'Croatoan' in the corridor hallway."

26

"What are you talking about?" asked Stanton. "Why do you say that?"

Lin cocked her head at the two men. "Were you not listening to her when she was arguing with you about poltergeists?"

"Just now?" Stanton asked.

"I don't think we were arguing exactly," added Mtumbe.

"No, not just now," Lin said. "Earlier, when you were ordering her over the comm links to open the equipment bay doors."

Stanton tried to remember. "What did she say exactly?"

"She was attempting to goad Lieutenant Petrov into more irrational responses," Lin recalled. "I could hear it all through my comm link. She listed all the unexplained happenings which might have been caused by a poltergeist."

"So?" asked Stanton.

"She listed the carved word together with the initial explosion and the nonworking entry pads," Lin explained.

Stanton just stared at her. He wasn't getting it.

"The word would not be an unexplained happening," Lin said in exasperation, "if she had actually done it. But in her own mind she has categorized it as unexplained and she accidentally admitted as much when she listed it among all the other things."

Stanton wasn't convinced. "She might have just been playing with Petrov," he said.

"Something I considered as well," Lin reported. "So after you had departed the equipment bay and Agent Gold was in the comm center, I quickly inspected the carving. This was while you were still yelling at her," she observed.

"Right," said Stanton. "There's an explanation for that."

"I assumed so," Lin replied politely. "In any event, I checked the carving and, knowing what to look for, there are obvious aging signs which indicate that it was carved well before our arrival."

"Are you sure?" Stanton asked.

"Yes, Captain," Lin replied confidently. "I was concerned about the information and so I made sure to be careful. Whatever was used, it was more then just a knife. The edges of the grooves were slightly rounded, indicating a heat source. More like a soldering gun or some such tool. In addition, the plastic coating around the letters was slightly scorched. More importantly, it had yellowed inside, indicating far more than a few minutes since the inside had been exposed to air."

Stanton nodded as Lin provided the explanation. He had no reason to doubt her and every reason to doubt Gold.

"Why would she say that?" he wondered aloud.

"What reason did she give you for doing it in the first

place?" Mtumbe asked. "That might shed some light on it."

Stanton frowned as he tried to remember. "I was about to report it back to Earth, when she took me aside and admitted—" he stopped himself and smiled darkly. "I mean, when she *claimed* she had been the one to carve it. I made her tell the whole crew, but it did stop me from comming back to Command."

"So she was willing to have the entire crew mad at her," observed Lin, "rather than have you send a communication back to Earth."

"Have we sent any communications back home yet?" Mtumbe asked.

"Yeah," Stanton nodded. "After you got hurt, when you were still in sick bay, I snuck onto the ship to send a comm back to Command."

"'Snuck'?" asked Mtumbe with a sideways glance. "How does a captain sneak onto his own ship?"

Stanton had to laugh, despite himself. "See, now, that's a good point. I was sneaking because I was trying to send the comm without Gold finding out. After I did the first round at your bedside I went to the ship instead of my quarters. I figured Gold would be asleep."

"And was she?" Mtumbe asked.

"No," answered Stanton. "She was already on the ship. She had just sent a comm back to Earth with an 'all clear' status. No mention of your infection, so Command wouldn't forbid us from coming home and starting a plague. I thought that was pretty smart of her actually."

Lin and Mtumbe looked at each other and shook their heads.

"Captain, are you certain she actually sent a

communication?" Lin asked. "Did you see her do it, or did she just tell you she had done it?"

Stanton's face grew grim. "You're right, Lin. I didn't see her do it. She told me she did, but I didn't see it."

"Just like she told you she had carved that word in the wall," Lin observed.

"So as far as we know," concluded Mtumbe ominously, "we've never sent any transmissions back to Earth."

"Just like the first colonists," Stanton mused. Then he considered the ramifications. "Was that her real assignment?" he posited. "To prevent any transmissions at all?"

There was no time for an answer because another question was being screamed down the access corridor. It was Rusakova, hurling aluminum plates and cups from the kitchen at Petrov who was running away from her, and toward them.

"How dare you?!" Rusakova was screaming hysterically. "How dare you?! How can you say such things, you monster?!"

27

"Shut up!" Rusakova screamed at Petrov. "Shut up, you devil!"

A cup bounced off Petrov's raised forearm and clattered to the floor. "You cannot shut up the truth, Oksana," he said, remarkably calm considering the attack he was enduring.

"I will shut you up, Aleksandr!" she shrieked. "You do not speak the truth! Your mouth spits only evil lies!"

Stanton rushed into the hallway to break it up and received a cup to the face for his trouble.

"Ow! Damn it!" he yelled, holding his left cheekbone. It was cut and blood started to seep from the wound.

Mtumbe had stepped into the doorway to monitor events. He pointed at his leader's injury. "Watch that. You don't want it to get infected."

Stanton glared at him.

"Oh, Captain," said Rusakova "I am so sorry. I did not mean to strike you."

"You meant to strike Petrov?" he asked, his hand to his

bleeding cheek.

"I mean to kill Petrov," growled Rusakova.

"There's been enough death today, Oksana," Stanton said.

"Do you think I do not know that?" Rusakova replied. "That is why I am so upset."

"Okay, okay," Stanton was starting to lose his patience. "Someone needs to tell me exactly what you two are fighting about."

"I am not fighting," Petrov insisted. "She is attacking me."

"You attack me with your words, Aleksandr!" shouted Rusakova.

"What words?" asked Stanton.

"He said Nils was to blame for his own death," Rusakova related. "He said that Nils deserved to die for angering the Martian gods at their temple."

Stanton turned to Petrov with an expression he hoped said, 'Did you really say that, and if so, what the hell is wrong with you?'

"I did not say he deserved to die," Petrov responded. "I said that he tempted the spirits and it is not surprising they punished him."

"That's a pretty slim distinction, Petrov," Stanton observed. "He died because his suit failed."

"Ah, yes, Captain." Petrov raised thick eyebrows over gaunt eyes. "But why did his suit fail?"

"His suit failed," Lin answered, "because of multiple points of fatigue, particularly at the joints and connections."

"That is *where* it failed," Petrov corrected, his eyes growing wider. "Not *why*."

Lin considered. "I am not sure I agree. The fatigue is the reason for the failure. It suggests excessive or extreme use of that particular suit."

"There are other explanations, my dear Lieutenant," Petrov grinned. "Less scientific, but equally valid. Perhaps more so."

"I think I'll stick with science," Lin responded. "It is superior to superstition."

"Today's science was yesterday's superstition," Petrov reminded her. "We're standing on what people used to think was the God of War moving across the night sky."

Lin thought for a moment. "I'm not sure how that means Dekker's suit failed for any reason other than excessive fatigue."

Petrov smiled broadly, a strange, disconcerting grin. "The evidence is all around you," he said. "You just refuse to accept it."

Just then Gold walked in. She seemed completely uninterested in the pending argument. Instead, she announced, "I've sent word of Dekker's death back to Command."

Mtumbe murmured, "Sure you did."

Before she could respond, Petrov said, "Agent Gold knows. She has kept track of all the dangers the spirits have inflicted upon us."

Rusakova's eyes widened at Gold. "You believe this lunatic? I thought you were smarter than that."

"I am," she said. She looked at Petrov. "What dangers? What are you talking about?"

"Do you not remember, Agent Gold?" said Petrov almost hypnotically. "When we were in the equipment bay, you listed all the misfortunes which have befallen us. You agreed they were committed by the poltergeist."

"Yeah, I wanted to talk to you about that list," said Stanton.

Gold ignored him to respond to Petrov. "I was joking, you idiot."

That seemed to shake Petrov.

"Stop it!" shouted Rusakova. "Shut up, all of you! This has nothing to do with a poltergeist! This about Nils! Nils!"

Everyone was shocked into silence.

"Nils died," she said, "because of a stupid senseless accident on this stupid senseless mission."

Then she narrowed her eyes and pointed at Stanton. "And because you took away the suit he was going to wear. If he'd worn that suit he'd still be alive!"

Stanton was stunned. "I— I'm not sure about that," he stammered.

"That is what I told her as well, Captain," Petrov said. "She blamed you, but I told her it would not have mattered what suit he wore. Whatever suit he was in would have been torn asunder when he angered the spirits."

"Shut up, Aleksandr!" shrieked Rusakova.

"No, everyone shut up!" bellowed Stanton. He'd had enough. "Dekker is dead because of an accident, plain and simple. He isn't dead because of spirits and he isn't dead because I took his suit away. Now everybody be quiet about it. The man deserves to be honored, not argued over."

There was a long awkward silence at the captain losing his temper. He wasn't one quick to anger, so when he did yell, it carried extra weight.

They may never like you, Ferguson had counseled him

once. *So be ready to make them fear you.*

"Yes, Captain," Rusakova was the first to break the silence. "Of course you are right. I would like to make arrangements for his memorial service."

"I apologize as well," Petrov said. "I will speak no more of this."

"I would like to run a full inspection of all the remaining suits and exogear," Lin suggested.

"Thank you, Lin," Stanton answered, his usual calm returning. "Those all sort of go together. We'll need to bury him outside. We can't cremate him. There's no oxygen outside for burning, and we're not doing it inside because of the health ramifications."

Stanton thought a bit more then added, "We'll need to do it today. We don't have a refrigerated morgue to slow decomposition."

Mtumbe was looking out of one of the corridor windows. "We might need a Plan B," he said grimly. "Here comes a sandstorm."

28

"Sandstorm?" confirmed Stanton as they all turned to look out the row of west-facing windows that ran the length of the main corridor. "Shit."

The storm was still distant but it was moving fast, and directly toward the station.

"Lin, please check shield status," Stanton instructed as they all watched the billowing dust cloud amass on the horizon.

Lin disappeared down the hallway and into the control center. After a moment she returned. "Shields fully operational."

That was a relief to Stanton.

"How long will the storm last?" Gold asked.

"Hard to say," answered Stanton.

"It could be a few minutes," Mtumbe added, "or it could be hours. Depends on how big the storm is."

Everyone looked out at the angry storm growing and swirling its way toward them.

"It looks very big," Rusakova said.

"Yes," agreed Petrov. Rusakova did not throw him a glare. Their spat was forgotten. This was far more serious.

"The worst part will be if it stops on top of us," Mtumbe went on. "These storms can rush across the open space at a hundred kilometers per hour, or they can stall out and spin and thrash in the same place for hours. It's like a hurricane over open sea. Sometimes they rush toward shore, sometimes they sit and spin for a while, growing stronger and bigger."

The storm was almost on them. In fact, the first grains of sand were beginning to strike the shields with an unmistakable buzzing zap noise. The midday sky was darkening too as a cloud of spinning dust began to arch overhead, blocking out the small, distant sun.

"We should move away from the windows," Stanton advised. "Just in case."

There were no disagreements and the entire crew made their way down the corridor and into the commissary. It was cramped but there were no windows, and if the storm did last for several hours, then they were already where the food and toilets were.

Petrov was murmuring to himself as they walked in and sat down. He was in his own world, but Stanton heard the words 'spirits' and 'mercy.'

"Knock it off, Petrov," Stanton ordered. "Don't start with the ghost stuff again."

Petrov's head jerked up and his darting eyes met the captain's. "Hush, Captain. Do not speak like that. I implore you."

"I'm not going to let you freak everyone out again," Stanton replied.

Petrov looked pained, nearly in agony. "No, no. I can hear them, Captain. They whisper to me. They promised they would not play any tricks until the storm had passed."

Stanton rolled his eyes. "Well, that's good, I suppose," he said sarcastically.

"Well, it was good," Petrov answered, "but you made them angry. They want us to believe in them, and you made them angry!"

Petrov stood up from the table and kicked the chair out behind him.

"Whoa, calm down, Petrov," Stanton said, standing up. Mtumbe stood up too and slowly took a position behind Petrov.

"Everything's going to be okay," Stanton soothed. He started wondering where they might be able to lock up Petrov until it was time to head home. "Just tell your spirit friends that everything is going to be okay."

Petrov tipped his head back, his dark eyes rolling within the deep eye sockets.

"They have stopped talking to me," he cried. "I can't hear them any more!"

And just then the power went out.

29

Although it was daytime, the sandstorm was blocking out most of the sunlight. In addition, they had moved inside to a windowless room. As a result, the loss of power resulted in almost complete darkness, with just a bit of faint light filtering in through the doorway from the corridor windows.

"Damn it!" yelled Stanton.

Mtumbe and Gold also added epithets. Rusakova started screaming and Petrov began reciting scripture in Russian. Lin remained silent.

"Quiet, everyone, quiet!" Stanton ordered after a moment. "Don't panic."

But once they were quiet, they had more reason to panic. The steady clicking of sand being incinerated by the shields had been replaced by the scratching, scraping, clawing noise of the sandstorm swallowing the station.

"You would not believe me!" yelled Petrov. "And now we will all pay the price!"

"I still don't believe you," Stanton said in the dark. "Lin, did your status check give any clues as to why the power failed?"

But she didn't answer.

"Lin?" Stanton called out. "Lin?"

Then there was a large electric pop, and the dim red emergency lighting turned on. They could see again, but Stanton almost wished they couldn't. Petrov's drawn face looked positively demonic in the crimson half light.

More importantly, though, the clicking buzz noise had returned. The shields were back on. A moment later, Lin walked back through the commissary door.

"The emergency power should have kicked in automatically," she complained. "I do not know why it didn't. But I went to the control center and activated it manually."

"How did you do that with the power off?" Gold asked, almost suspiciously. "Wouldn't the control glass have been off too?"

Lin smiled, allowing her bemusement to appear on her scarlet lit features. "There is a manual switch in the wall in the control room," she explained. "You really should familiarize yourself with the station's blueprints, Agent Gold."

Gold just sneered at Lin.

"So now what?" asked Rusakova.

"Now we wait for the storm to pass," answered Stanton.

"And hope the shields hold," added Mtumbe.

Everyone expected Petrov to make some comment about not angering the great and powerful spirits of Mars. But he didn't.

In fact, Stanton couldn't see him anywhere in the dim red light of the commissary.

"Petrov?"

"Aleksandr?"

A quick search of the room confirmed it.

"He's gone!"

30

"Aw, crap," said Stanton. "This is not good."

"We must find him," warned Rusakova. "There is no telling what he might do."

"Let's split into teams," Gold suggested. Then she looked over at Stanton. "Unless you think that's a bad idea, Captain?"

Stanton was stunned at even being asked. It was a day of surprises. "No, Agent Gold," he replied. "It's a good idea."

He turned to Rusakova. "Where do you think he might have gone, Oksana?"

"Who knows?" she answered. "He is crazy."

"Not very helpful," Stanton said. "Try again."

"The entry bay?" she suggested. "To get back on the ship again?"

"Okay, that makes sense," Stanton answered. "You and Gold go there."

Then he threw the question open to everyone. "Where else?"

"The control center," suggested Lin. "To turn off the

emergency power?"

"Good," said Stanton. "You and Mtumbe go there."

"Where are you going?" Mtumbe asked him.

Stanton's features hardened in the dim scarlet light. "Sickbay," he answered. "If he's obsessed with ghosts and death, he might try to do something to Dekker's body."

31

Stanton walked into the sick bay but had to stop suddenly. Dekker had only been dead for a few hours, but the smell—*that* smell—was already starting.

He had been around dead bodies before. It came with the territory. Exploring space is dangerous work and not everyone makes it. When he was training on the Moon Base, one of the older astronauts had gotten himself electrocuted. It was a month before the next transport. They finally had just put the body outside, but not before everyone became acquainted with the smell of death.

Remember that smell, Junior, Ferguson had told him. *There's a reason it makes your stomach turn and you have to fight the urge to run away. It reminds us we're all mortal. And when you can smell it, that means it's close. Really close. And you know you might be next.*

Stanton stepped all the way into the infirmary. The dim red light illuminated Dekker's naked body eerily. Red-black shadows curved into the crevices of his corpse. All of the blood had settled in the bottom of the body, leaving the top a sickly paste-pink. His eyelids had been closed, but not even

Stanton could shake that B-movie feeling that Dekker would suddenly open his eyes and grab him in the iron grip zombies apparently gained in death.

He circled the entire room silently, inspecting the walls and furniture. He avoided the table with Dekker's remains. Instead he checked everything else in a methodical clockwise sweep of the room. It was only when he had finished that sweep that he walked over to the foot of the metal table supporting what used to be Nils Dekker, and said, "Okay, come out from under the table, Petrov."

There was a pause, but then Petrov emerged from the blackness under the table. He stood up in the red gloom of the sick bay.

"You saw me," he said.

"No," replied Stanton. "I guessed. But I guessed right."

Petrov was visibly upset, even in the half light. "I should have stayed under there," he cursed himself.

"Well, I would have checked before leaving," Stanton answered. "It's not like there are a lot of places to hide in here."

Stanton walked over and sat on one of the three small chairs in the sick bay. "We need to talk, Aleksandr."

Petrov lowered his head. "Yes. Yes, we do."

He didn't take one of the chairs, but instead sat on the other metal examining table.

"Why did you come here?" Stanton asked. "And please tell me you weren't going to defile Dekker's remains."

"Defile?" Petrov repeated indignantly. "Of course not. Nils was my friend." Then he added poignantly, "He was the only one who believed me."

Stanton smiled in the red light. "I want to believe you, Aleksandr," he started. "Well, no. I actually don't want to believe you. I don't want to believe that on top of everything else we have to deal with—missing colonists, missing comm equipment, sandstorms—I don't want to believe that we also have to worry about ghosts haunting the station trying to kill us. And I don't want to believe that Dekker died because he jumped up on that rock and made a bad joke."

Petrov shook his head. "That is never what I said. Oksana did not understand what I was trying to say. I only wanted her to believe me. I am not crazy, Captain, I swear it."

Stanton nodded patiently. "I know, I know. And I'll admit that I don't understand everything there is to know in this universe. When I was a little kid, not more than eight, I had a dream that my grandmother, who lived across the country, came and sat on my bed. She told me what a good kid I was and how she was so proud of who I was and what I'd become some day. I found out the next day that she had died that night."

Petrov smiled, his teeth gleaming pink in the emergency light. "That was no dream," he nodded.

Stanton shrugged. "I don't know. But at least I know that I don't know. So I'm open to what you're saying. But you have got to understand, Aleksandr, you're freaking everybody out. And it doesn't help matters that when the power cut out you snuck away to hang out with a corpse."

Petrov's eyebrows shot up. "Oh no, Captain. That is not what happened at all. When the power went out, I knew it was because of the poltergeist—"

"Petrov..." Stanton warned.

"Hear me out, Captain, please. When the power went out, I knew it was the poltergeist playing a trick on us. I could feel it. But I also knew that it was very, very dangerous.

Sometimes the spirits do not understand what mortal danger they put us in."

"You're losing me here, Aleksandr," said Stanton. "Bring it back to reality."

"I knew the sandstorm could damage, even destroy the station with the shields off," Petrov continued. "So I rushed out of the commissary and straight to the control center to engage the manual override switch for the emergency power."

"Okay. See, now I know you're lying," interrupted Stanton. "Lin is the one who flipped that switch."

"I don't doubt it, Captain," answered Petrov, "for when I entered the control center and attempted to locate the switch in the complete blackness, the spirits carried me through the walls to the sick bay. They wanted me to be here, close to them."

"All right, Aleksandr. You just lost me. You were transported here by spirits?"

"Yes, Captain," Petrov practically pleaded. "I know it sounds insane, but you must believe me. I went to open the wall cabinet for the manual override switch, but instead I found myself in the darkest of worlds, not knowing which way was which, following the blackness before my nose. I felt as if I were falling, falling forward forever and ever, and then, when the red auxiliary power lights turned on, I was here, in the sick bay, with Nils."

Stanton just stared at him.

"Nils needed me to come to him, I think," explained Petrov. "Perhaps to tell me he did not blame me for what I said. But I also felt he had something to tell us. Something about the spirits who wish to do us harm. So I began meditating to try to communicate with him. That's when I heard your footsteps in the corridor. I didn't know who, or what, it was, and so I became frightened and hid under the table. I am sorry for my cowardice, Captain."

Stanton stared at the Russian. It was a lot to take in all at once.

"Do you believe me, Captain?" Petrov looked him the eyes, his own troubled and haunted.

Stanton managed a grimace. "I don't think you're lying," he said. "But I don't believe you either."

He sighed deeply, then leaned forward and put a hand on his crewman's arm. "You've become a danger to the rest of the crew, Aleksandr. Will you agree to being confined to quarters?"

32

Petrov opened his mouth to reply, then shut it again and looked up.

"Do you hear that?" he asked is a desperate, raspy voice.

"No more ghost stories, Aleksandr," Stanton warned.

Petrov shook his head violently. "No, no. Not that. The click-clack of the sand hitting the shields. It has changed."

To Stanton, the constant buzzing of incinerated sand molecules had faded into background noise. Sensory adaptation had rendered it essentially inaudible, but he refocused and he could clearly hear what Petrov described. The shields weren't destroying the sand overhead any more. They could both hear the sand smashing directly against the metal roof of the sick bay.

"Let's get back to the control center," Stanton said. "Maybe one of your poltergeists blew the switch again."

They hurried to the control room where Mtumbe and Lin were sitting against each other in the dim light. When Stanton walked in, Mtumbe jumped up.

"We were just talking!"

Lin stood up slowly and just smiled.

"Not interested right now, Daniel," said Stanton. "The auxiliary power is failing. We need to check the switch."

"The switch is fine," Lin reported. "We checked it a few minutes ago and it is still connected."

Reinspection confirmed this.

"Listen again, Captain," said Petrov. "The shields are working in here."

Sure enough, the buzzing of incinerated sand was clearly audible in the control room.

"Damn it," said Stanton. "That means the shields are starting to fail selectively."

"What do you mean?" asked Mtumbe.

"The shields aren't working over the sick bay," Stanton clarified.

"That could threaten the entire station," Lin realized.

"I know," answered Stanton. "We need to get the shields up again. They may be failing elsewhere as well."

Just then Gold and Rusakova walked in. "No sign of Petrov," Gold reported before seeing him.

"I have found me," he grinned. "Right here."

"Great," answered Gold. "So it was you who sabotaged our emergency power?"

"On the contrary," he explained, "I was on my way to activate the emergency power when the spirits transported me to sick bay."

Gold stared at him for a moment then turned to Stanton. "You need to lock him up," she said.

"I'm working on it," he replied. "In the meantime we have a serious situation. The shields have failed over the sickbay. The station roof there is getting ravaged by the sandstorm."

"What can we do about it?" Rusakova asked.

"We could ask the spirits for help," Petrov suggested.

Gold looked again at Stanton. "Seriously. Locked up."

Stanton gave a tight smile. "Seriously. Working on it."

"We could try diverting some of the power to the shields there," Lin suggested. "But I don't know if the control glass is fully operational at emergency power levels."

"Plus, if there is finite power available," Rusakova pointed out, "diverting power there might weaken the shields elsewhere."

Stanton thought for a moment. "Rusakova, how's the ship holding up?"

"It seemed fine, Captain," she answered. "It was built for the vacuum of space. I believe it will withstand some sand."

"Are you thinking we could divert some of the power from the ship to get all shields operational?" Mtumbe asked.

"Bad idea," said Gold. "That ship is our ticket home. We shouldn't do anything to endanger it."

"Well, then," started Mtumbe, "what are we going to—"

But his question was interrupted by the deafening buzz of the station's emergency alarm.

33

Dzzzt! Dzzzt! Dzzzt!

Stanton and the others could barely hear each other over the alarm.

"Oh my God! What's happening?" shouted Rusakova.

Petrov fell to the ground, holding his ears and screaming, "Stop it! Stop it!"

Mtumbe and Stanton both covered their ears against the noise and looked for some indication of catastrophic failure.

Lin ignored the alarm and began manipulating the control glass for information. Gold, too, was nonplussed by the alarm and peeked over Lin's shoulder. After a moment she straightened up and walked out of the control room, tapping Stanton on the chest as she passed and motioning for him to follow her.

He did. And so did Mtumbe, but not before yelling over the din of the alarm for Lin and Rusakova to stay with Petrov, who was balled up on the floor, and screaming, "The spirits are angry! The spirits are angry!"

The alarm was just as loud in the corridor, so Stanton

didn't bother yelling after Gold about where she was leading them. But it only took a minute to see for himself.

A fortified blast shield had already descended across the end of the corridor, completely sealing off the sickbay from the rest of the station.

"There must have been a hull breech," shouted Stanton. "The station autosealed that section off."

Gold nodded in agreement. "Is there any way through that wall?"

"No," replied Stanton. "That wall is designed for safety. It comes down to hermetically seal off that section from the rest of the station. The only way back in would be to go outside and down through the emergency roof access each room has."

Then Stanton realized something. "Damn it," he said. "Dekker is in there."

Mtumbe realized something too. "So are my antibiotics."

34

The alarm stopped as suddenly as it had started. Stanton's ears rang in the ensuing silence. The lights didn't come back on, though, so they were left in the red gloom while the sandstorm continued to rage over their heads.

"When was your last dose?" Stanton asked Mtumbe.

"This morning with breakfast," Mtumbe frowned. "Next dose is supposed to be with dinner."

Stanton saw Gold lean away from Mtumbe just a bit. She saw him looking at her, so she took a full step back as if appraising Mtumbe's leg. "How's it healing, Commander?"

Mtumbe hesitated at the unexpected question from an unexpected source.

"I think it's fine," Mtumbe answered. "A little numb to the touch, but it doesn't hurt. In fact, I don't think I need the antibiotics any more anyway."

Stanton almost believed him.

"No," said Stanton. "We'll figure something out. Anyway, I don't want to leave Dekker's body in there too long. Assuming we can repair whatever damage breeched the hull, we don't want the entire sick bay fouled by a decomposing body."

"Especially one that's now exposed to Martian air," Mtumbe raised his leg in illustration. "They got some nasty bugs here on the Red Planet."

"Mars needs antibiotics," joked Gold dryly.

Stanton smiled. He just couldn't stay mad at her.

Then Lin came running up to them, clearly agitated. She was rarely agitated.

"Come quickly," she said. "It's Petrov."

They followed her back to the control room where they found Petrov laying on the floor apparently unconscious. Rusakova was kneeling beside him, a hand on his chest.

"Is he okay?" asked Stanton. "What's wrong?"

"I am not sure," Rusakova replied. "He was holding his head and complaining about the spirit voices. Then all of a sudden, he jerked his head back, his eyes rolled up into his head, and he went limp."

"He's not dead, is he?" Gold asked.

"No," replied Lin. "His pulse and breathing are normal. He's just unresponsive."

"We should move Petrov to sick bay," suggested Rusakova.

"Negative," replied Stanton. "Sick bay is inaccessible. The storm breeched the hull there so it's been autosealed off. We can't get inside until we send a crew to repair the breech."

Lin looked with concern, first at Mtumbe's leg, then to his face. "Your antibiotics are in there."

"Don't worry," he smiled. "I'll be all right."

Her face showed she didn't believe him either.

"Let's move him to his quarters," said Stanton. "We can

lay him on his cot until we figure out what's going on."

They returned to the control room and Stanton grabbed a hold of Petrov under the arms. Mtumbe tried to lift the Russian's feet, but he couldn't put much weight on his injured leg. Lin pushed him out of the way, and she and Gold each grabbed a leg. Mtumbe and Rusakova followed behind.

As they all headed toward the sleeping quarters, Stanton heard Rusakova whisper to Mtumbe, "Nils's body is still in sick bay, isn't it?"

Mtumbe frowned. "I'm afraid so."

Rusakova shook her head. "He was a good man. He deserves a proper burial."

Mtumbe patted her on the shoulder. "Captain Stanton is a good man too. He'll make sure Nils gets a decent burial."

They arrived at the sleeping cabins and laid Petrov on his bed. As they stepped back, Petrov began to stir slightly. His rolled back and forth. Then his eyelids popped open, but his eyes were still rolled back into his skull.

"Leave," he moaned in an otherworldly voice. "Leave this place, or suffer the fate of your predecessors."

35

"Petrov!" Stanton shook the transfixed Russian. "Petrov, snap out of it!"

Petrov didn't seem to respond to the captain. Instead his eyes rolled around in his head and he started saying, "Croatoan, Croatoan," over and over.

Stanton threw a harsh glance at Gold, who looked back quizzically.

"Petrov," Stanton said more calmly, almost soothingly. "Petrov, can you hear me?"

Gold rolled her eyes at the captain, but Rusakova seemed genuinely concerned. Mtumbe and Lin looked at each other.

"Is he trying to humor him?" Lin whispered to Mtumbe.

"I'm not really sure," Mtumbe whispered back. "Let's see what happens."

"Petrov," the captain repeated. "Aleksandr? It's John. We're all here, Aleksandr."

Petrov's eyes regained their focus and he looked at

Stanton's face. "Captain?"

"Yes, Aleksandr, it's me."

"I'm scared, Captain," Petrov said.

"I know, Aleksandr."

"They want us to leave, Captain."

"Who do?" Stanton asked. "Who wants us to leave?"

"The spirits, Captain," answered Petrov, still dreamlike. "They say we are disturbing their rest and we need to leave."

"Oh, brother," muttered Gold.

Stanton shushed her.

"Aleksandr," he went on, "tell them we need to find out what happened to our friends, and then we'll leave."

Petrov was silent for a moment, then he said, "They say if we don't leave, then what happened to them will happen to us."

Stanton could hear Ferguson mocking him. *He's crazy, Junior. Just lock him up and get on with your mission.*

"Aleksandr," he pressed on. "Ask them what happened to our friends."

Petrov didn't reply. Stanton waited for a moment, then repeated, "Petrov? Petrov?"

But he had had become unresponsive again.

Stanton threw his hands up in frustration.

Mtumbe pulled him aside, "I know you're trying to humor him, but you're starting to freak everybody else out. You don't think he's really talking to ghosts do you?"

"No," Stanton insisted. "No, of course not. He's clearly delusional. Probably some schizophrenic break. But if I can get him to resolve it within his own reality, I think he's more likely to accept the confinement we're going to have to put him under."

Mtumbe looked at his friend for a few moments. "And that's all this is?"

Stanton smiled. "That's all this is."

"Really?"

"Really."

Mtumbe smiled broadly. "Good. You had me worried for a second there."

Then Petrov started to speak again. His voice was frail and distant. "Wh— Where am I?" he rasped.

"You are in your cabin," Rusakova answered.

Petrov pushed himself up on one elbow. "Is the emergency passed? The alarm is off."

"It's over for now," Stanton answered. "But we have other problems."

The most obvious was that the main power had not yet come on. They were still bathed in pale red light.

"I don't remember anything after the alarm started," Petrov said.

"Nothing at all?"

Petrov thought for a moment. "Not really. But I have an image in my head."

Just then, the power snapped back on. Regular lighting was finally restored. Rusakova and Gold stepped toward the window to check on the status of the sandstorm.

"What's the image in your head, Petrov?" Stanton asked.

"It's the station," Petrov explained as he clenched his eyes shut and rubbed his temples. "Er, no, it's not the station. Well, it's fourteen astronauts in the station."

"Fourteen?" Stanton asked.

Petrov's face screwed up into a pained grimace. "Yes,

Captain. But the station is built on top of a cemetery. And the fourteen astronauts are all dead."

Lin considered for a moment. "There were only seven colonists."

"And there are seven of us," Mtumbe realized. "Fourteen."

"Did you say the station was on top of a cemetery?" Stanton asked Petrov to confirm.

But before he could answer, Rusakova and Gold returned.

"You're not going to believe this," Gold announced.

"What?" asked Stanton on behalf of all of them.

"The sandstorm moved a great deal of sand outside," explained Rusakova. "It uncovered something."

"What?" asked Stanton again.

Petrov didn't say anything but he looked up at Stanton with haunted eyes.

"Large stones," answered Rusakova. "Just like we found out there. Only—"

"Only they're directly beneath the station," finished Stanton.

"Hey," said Gold. "How did you know that?"

Stanton didn't answer. Mtumbe and Lin just looked at each other. And Petrov put his head in his hands and started to sob.

36

Gold looked down at Petrov. "I missed something, didn't I?"

"He said he had a vision," Lin explained. "Fourteen dead astronauts inside a space station built on a cemetery."

"A cemetery?" Rusakova asked.

"Think 'burial ground,'" said Mtumbe.

Gold looked around. "And why fourteen astronauts?"

"Our crew plus the original colonists," Stanton explained. "But it's the ravings of a deeply troubled man, and nothing to take seriously."

He knelt down next to Petrov and placed a gentle hand on his quivering shoulder. "Aleksandr, we have some work to do now that the storm is over. I'm ordering you to stay in your cabin. Do you think you can follow that order?"

Petrov gave an exaggerated nod, but didn't quite lift his head from his hands.

"Okay, good man," said Stanton. Then he stood up and addressed the rest of the crew. "Staff meeting," he announced. He pointed across the hall. "Commissary. Let's go."

"We can see his cabin from here," Stanton explained to Mtumbe in a low voice as they walked. "Keep an eye out to make sure he doesn't leave."

Mtumbe nodded. "Will do."

When they got to the commissary, everyone took a seat, except for Stanton who stood to address his crew.

"We need to all get on the same page," he began. "A lot of things have happened since we arrived. A lot of bad things. We've lost one crew member—"

Rusakova fought back a sob.

"—and another one," Stanton continued, motioning back toward Petrov's room, "is essentially out of commission as well. Not to mention Commander Mtumbe's injury. That leaves four and a half of us to do the work of seven. And now we have even more work to do.

"In addition to our primary goal of determining what happened to the first crew, we also need to properly dispose of Dekker's remains."

"Yes," said Rusakova simply.

"But to do that," Stanton went on, "we need to get into the sick bay. Luckily, we need to do that anyway because Mtumbe's antibiotics are in there."

"I think I'll be okay," Mtumbe offered.

"Not a chance I want to take," Stanton responded. "And not just because I want you to heal up. The last thing we need is a Martian disease spreading among us.

"On top of all that, we need to keep Petrov safe and secure so he doesn't try to open the airlock to let the voices in his head go for a walk."

"So what's the plan?" Mtumbe asked.

"We're going to have to split into teams," Stanton said.

"First priority is a Marswalk to inspect the damage from the sandstorm. If it's easily repairable, that same team will also repair the breech to sick bay. Even if it's not easily repairable, the team needs to enter sick bay by way of the emergency roof access to retrieve Mtumbe's antibiotics."

"What about Nils's body?" Rusakova asked.

"That's more difficult," Stanton admitted. "It's not really going to be possible to lift the body up and out of sick bay through the roof access. It's difficult enough just to lift a body, it won't be possible to raise it three meters off the ground while wearing a spacesuit."

"If the breech can be repaired," said Stanton, "then we repair it and restore access through the station to move the body out through the west airlock. If it can't be repaired, we remove everything we need from sick bay and we will just have to leave his body there, I'm afraid."

Rusakova looked down but didn't say anything. She understood the situation.

"What is the second priority, Captain?" Lin asked.

"I want to know why we lost main power," the captain answered, "and whether that's likely to happen again."

"What about the ship?" asked Gold.

"I feel good about the ship," Stanton replied, "but you're right. We need to confirm it's in good shape too. If not, that would become the overwhelming priority. So one team will be outside checking for damage from the storm and recovering what we need from sick bay. The other team will be inside, checking on the ship and station power levels and doing a full diagnostic."

"There are two more concerns," Lin said.

"Yes," answered Stanton. "One is Petrov."

"How do we watch him?" Lin asked.

Stanton sighed. "The planners of this station didn't foresee the need for a jail," he lamented. "I suppose that speaks well of all of us, in a way. But it means we'll have to have someone dedicated to watching him, reducing the rest of the team down to just four. Two outside and two inside."

"What's the last concern?" Mtumbe asked.

Stanton shrugged. "After we make sure we're all safe, we need to see whether Petrov was right."

"Right about what?" asked Gold.

Stanton's expression hardened. "Is the station built on top of a Martian burial ground?"

37

"Okay, you know that's crazy, right?" Gold said.

"What I know," answered Stanton, "is one of my crew is dead, one is injured, and the another one is either nuts or psychic."

"He's nuts," assured Gold.

"Maybe not," admitted Rusakova. "There are many people from Aleksandr's part of Russia who claim to be able to communicate with the spirit world."

Gold just looked at her. When Rusakova refused to return her stare, Gold looked at Stanton, but he just shrugged.

"I don't think we can just dismiss it out of hand any more," Stanton said. "That's what we did at first and look where we are now."

"What are you talking about?" Gold said. "No one was talking about ghosts when we got here."

"Well, we can talk later about why that might be," said Stanton.

Gold cocked her head at the captain, so he repeated, "Later."

"Well, I can't speak for Petrov," Mtumbe interrupted the ensuing awkward silence, "but I feel a lot better now. Totally healthy."

Stanton looked at him with a bemused smile.

"Really," assured Mtumbe. "You can cross me off the injured list."

"Don't be so brave," Lin chided him. "Your leg is still weak and you likely still have that infection in you. You are not only injured, you are ill."

Mtumbe opened his mouth to argue, but Stanton interrupted. "She's right, Daniel. Which is why we need to get outside and to sick bay as soon as possible."

He looked out the commissary window and considered. Mars had approximately the same axial tilt as Earth, meaning it had the same seasons. They were in late fall, so the days—which were already only 23 hours—were starting to have even less daylight hours. The sandstorm had chewed up the better part of the afternoon. If they went out now, there was a good chance the sun would set before they finished everything they needed to do: inspect the ship, inspect the entire station, locate the hull breech, fix the hull breech, retrieve the antibiotics, and inspect the alleged burial ground. That was too much. Better prioritize.

"We'll do a quick run to sick bay to get the antibiotics," he announced. "If we're lucky we'll figure out where the hull breech is, maybe even fix it. But then we'd better get indoors for the night. Tomorrow we'll do a full inspection of the station, the ship, and the burial ground."

"Sounds like a plan," Mtumbe said. "So who's the 'we' that gets to go exploring?"

"Me," and answered Stanton, "and Gold."

"Me?" Gold asked, but Stanton gave her a stony glare. "Right. Me."

"Lin and Rusakova will do an internal diagnostic on the station and the ship," Stanton went on.

They each nodded and offered a "Yes, sir."

"What about me?" Mtumbe asked.

Stanton smiled again. "You're still too weak to go on a spacewalk. And I don't want you hobbling all around doing a diagnostic. So you, my friend, get to guard Petrov."

Mtumbe slapped his forehead. "Guard duty? How boring."

Stanton raised an eyebrow. "You'd better hope so."

38

"Did you double check the suit?" Gold asked as Lin sealed her helmet.

"I triple checked it," Lin replied. "There are no weaknesses or stressed areas. It is perfectly safe."

Stanton smiled through his helmet glass at Rusakova. He knew he didn't need to ask. She smiled back—a tight, worried, but controlled smile that assured him she had also thoroughly checked his suit.

Two minutes later, Stanton and Gold were exiting the other end of the west airlock out onto the Martian surface. They had their comm links activated between them, but Stanton had insisted the comm feed back to the comm center not be activated. They would check in if need be. He had said it was to conserve power. He knew no one believed him.

The sandstorm had been awesome. There were giant windswept dunes of orange sand piled against the station. The dunes were especially high in the corners and crevices of the station's outside walls, some well taller than Stanton and Gold. In conjunction, there were sections of the ground which looked like they had been scooped out with an excavator. It was in one of these ditches that Gold and Lin had seen the rectangular stones like the ones Dekker had spotted.

"There they are," Gold said to Stanton over the comm link.

Stanton nodded and stepped over to them. There was no doubt that they matched the standing stones. They were approximately the same size and shape. The only difference was that these were all laying on their sides, and had, prior to the windstorm, all been covered by the Martian ground. There were three that he could make out, lined up like pick-up sticks, but there could easily be more farther under the sand, unexposed by the storm.

"Is this what you saw out there?" Gold asked.

"Yes and no," Stanton answered. "We saw stones like these, but they were erect."

Gold looked demurely through her helmet. "Pardon me, Captain? Did you say 'erect.'"

Stanton blushed, visible even through the gold tint of the helmet glass. "Wow, Agent Gold. Are we in middle school again?"

Gold laughed. "Not hardly," she replied. "I wasn't anywhere near as confident and collected back then."

Stanton smiled. "I bet you were," he replied. "You just didn't know it."

Gold shook her head. "No, I was the homely, brainy girl who no one would talk to. And who still hated going home at the end of each school day."

"I can believe the brainy part," Stanton remarked, "but looking at you now, I can't imagine you were ever homely."

Gold fought back a blush of her own. She distracted

with a joke. "It's the spacesuit," she said. "I look great in spacesuits."

Stanton laughed. "Come on. We'll look at the stones on our way back, if we have time. But our priority has to be Daniel's antibiotics."

Gold agreed and they hurried past the uncovered ruins toward the sick bay module.

It was eerily quiet. There was little noise on the windswept planet. What sounds there might be, rushing wind or rocks being blown onto each other, could only manage weak sound waves in the thin atmosphere, dying a gentle death against the metal casing of the astronauts' helmets.

Stanton filled the silence.

"So why did you lie about carving 'Croatoan' in the wall?"

Gold almost choked. "Wh— I— Wh— What are you talking about?" she finally managed to ask.

"I know you didn't carve 'Croatoan' in the corridor support post," Stanton replied, almost casually. "I just don't know why."

"Of course I did it," Gold insisted. "I told you that. And I told you why. It was a test."

Stanton shrugged inside his spacesuit. "So was this," he said, a bit sadly.

They trudged in silence from that point until they had reached the sick bay module.

Stanton pointed at the ladder and motioned for her to go up first. He could have said as much, but he didn't really feel like talking to her just then. Gold grabbed a hold of the ladder and began the climb to the top. Stanton followed but this time he didn't look at her spacesuit-covered behind.

When they reached the top, they moved to the center of the module where the emergency access hatch was. This didn't require a computer access pad. It was old-fashioned steel-meets-steel. All they needed to get in was enough strength to turn the wheel-like handle to unlock the porthole.

Stanton knelt down and tried to spin the wheel, but it didn't move at all. He pushed and pulled and struggled against the wheel but he couldn't get it to move. His vain grunts echoed in their comm links.

Without saying anything, Gold knelt down opposite him and grabbed the wheel as well, each of her hands between each of his.

Stanton looked her in the eye for a moment, then looked down and tried to turn the wheel again. Gold added her strength and after a moment, they could feel the wheel start to budge. The budge turned to a move, then to a turn. Gold let go and Stanton spun the wheel all the way open. He pulled open the hatch door, exposing the interior ladder along the far wall of the sick bay.

"After you," Stanton said simply.

Gold smiled weakly. "Thank you, Captain."

She stepped around and then began lowering herself carefully into the sick bay. At the bottom she landed with a clank on the hard metal floor.

When Stanton joined her with a clank of his own, he scanned the room and noticed the same thing that Gold had also noticed judging by the utter astonishment on her face.

Dekker's body was gone.

39

"Wh— Where's the body?" Gold asked. "This is where it was, right?"

Stanton stepped over to the examining table where they had laid Dekker's body that very morning. He circled it, one gloved hand remaining loosely atop the table. "Yes," he finally answered, tapping on the metal table. "This is it. Right here."

Stanton looked around the room. Not for the body. He knew it hadn't just walked over to one of the chairs in the corner. He just looked. For something, anything, to help explain.

"Somebody must have moved it," Gold concluded.

Stanton shook his head. "Not unless it was you and Rusakova. I came straight from here to the command center with Petrov. When we left, the body was still here. We went straight to the command center where Mtumbe and Lin were. Then you and Rusakova showed up."

Gold looked around too, the concern creasing her brow.

"Was there any time you and Rusakova were separated?" Stanton asked.

Gold frowned. "Do you think she moved the body?"

"Well, did you do it?" he countered.

"No," Gold shot back immediately. "Of course not."

Stanton shrugged. "I guess she might have tried to move it. Maybe to say goodbye and, I don't know. Maybe get him buried or outside or something?"

Gold nodded. "Get him outside to help preserve the body in the cold until a funeral could be arranged?"

Stanton shook his head again. "It doesn't really add up. Why do that? It's not like we weren't going to do it."

"Love can be a strange emotion," Gold offered. "People can do some apparently illogical things."

Stanton was surprised. "Personal experience?" he asked.

"None of your business, Captain," Gold smiled. "Just trying to make a point. And maybe explain the disappearance of an eighty-kilogram body."

Stanton scanned the room for clues. He wished he could rub his chin in thought but the helmet prevented it. "So there was a time you were separated from Rusakova?"

Gold frowned as she considered the question. "I think the only time was when we were on the ship still. Once it was pretty clear Petrov wasn't there, we split up for a few minutes to finish the search of the last sections of the ship. The engine room, storage, stuff like that."

"But that was while you were still on the ship?" Stanton asked.

"Yes," replied Gold. "And it was only for a few minutes. I don't see how she could have gone through the airlock, moved the body—by herself, by the way—and gotten back onto the ship in that short of time."

"Well, the only other explanation," said Stanton, "is that Dekker reanimated and walked off on his own."

"I'm not sure I like the idea of a zombie astronaut," Gold said.

"I was just trying to make a point," answered the captain. "I think we can safely rule out the undead. That leaves the Rusakova scenario. What was it Sherlock Holmes once said? 'Once you've eliminated the impossible, what remains, however improbable,' or something like that?"

Gold laughed at the captain's inarticulateness. "Something like that."

Stanton smiled at Gold, glad to share the moment, then he remembered where he was, and why.

"We should get back," he gruffed. "Help me find Mtumbe's antibiotics."

Gold nodded and they did a sweep of the sickbay. "Here they are," announced Gold holding up a bottle of pills from the counter. "Did he have more?"

"No, just those from the ship," Stanton answered. "The sick bay was all out, remember?"

"Right," said Gold, and she dropped the pill bottle into her suit's pouch. "I guess we can go now."

Stanton was standing in the middle of the room, doing his best, within the constraints of the suit, to look up at the ceiling.

"What is it?" Gold asked.

"Just looking for the hull breech," Stanton answered. "I don't see anything."

"Oh," said Gold.

"It's probably just too small to see," Stanton went on. "Maybe a tear at a seam or something. Too bad almost."

"Why too bad?" asked Gold.

"If it were a hole in the roof, at least we'd know right away and could fix it quickly," Stanton explained. "If it's just a tiny tear in some coupling, it's going to take forever to find it. I don't think we'll have enough time to fix it. That means we've lost the sick bay."

Gold considered the captain's comment. "How much time do you think we have?"

"If the first crew had been here," he started, "if this all had just been a simple communications issue, we would have had 18 months, like the original plan. But now..."

He raised his space-suited arms and motioned at the sickbay and the station beyond. "Now we know we're going back to Earth. The only question is how long we stay while we try to figure out what happened to the first crew. We've lost one of our crew already. Another is injured and sick. Another is losing his mind. And we haven't even been here two days yet."

"So why don't we just head home now?" Gold suggested.

"Because that's not our mission," Stanton was ready with his reply. He'd been thinking about it already. "Our mission was either to relieve the first crew if they were okay, or, if they weren't, to find out why. They aren't, so our mission is to find out why."

Gold nodded inside her helmet. "Agreed. But you haven't answered the question. How much time do you think we have?"

"Ordinarily we would have had about ten days before

Mars and Earth started to get too far apart to be able to get back home again," Stanton answered. "That's what I had in my head when we landed. Ten days, and we could stretch it to twelve or thirteen if we really had to."

He threw his arms wide again. "But with everything that's happening, I don't think we'll last ten days. How can we keep Petrov under guard for eight more days without a brig? How can we treat Mtumbe's infection for eight more days without a sick bay? How can we live eight more days in a haunted space station?"

Gold was struck by the word. "Haunted? Did you really just say the station is haunted?"

Stanton shrugged in his suit. "It's built on some ancient Martian burial ground or something. We've been inundated with unexplainable mishap after unexplainable mishap, and the psychic cosmonaut from the haunted Russian village is hearing spirit voices and having visions."

Gold just looked at him through her helmet.

"Or else it's all just a coincidence," Stanton laughed. "And a whole lot of bad luck."

It took a moment for Gold to formulate her response.

"I would think the captain of a space ship would be a scientist above all," she said, "and would draw conclusions based on facts and observations, not superstitions and fears."

Stanton figured she expected him to respond negatively. Instead, he smiled.

"Facts, huh?" he asked.

"Yes," Gold affirmed.

"Then why don't you stop lying to me?"

40

"Lying to you?" stammered Gold. "I don't know what you mean."

"I mean," grinned Stanton. "That I know you didn't carve 'Croatoan' in the corridor wall. And until you admit that and tell me why you lied to the entire crew, it's going to be hard to trust you, let alone explain my decisions."

Gold looked at him, unsure what to say.

"In fact," he went on, "as long as you lie and mislead, it's impossible for me to have the information I need to make the right decisions for our team."

Gold's expression changed slightly, from no expression at all to one of the slightest consideration.

"One person is already dead, Gold. How many more need to die before you'll actually be part of this team?"

"You can't lay Dekker's death at my feet, Captain."

"I can and I will," Stanton replied. "Part of the reason we even went out there was because Dekker saw the stone formation and told Petrov. That convinced Petrov there were ghosts on Mars and he stared freaking out. So we went to see what it really was. I was expecting an interesting, but natural rock formation. Not Mars Henge."

Gold stared Stanton in the eyes, her own hardening into tight slits. "You told me you were looking for the missing comm equipment."

Stanton paused. Finally he said, "Hm. How about that?"

"So you lied to me too."

"I don't know who I can trust," Stanton explained.

"You mean you don't trust me."

"I want to trust you," Stanton said, "but you're giving me reasons not to."

"Well, then let's get back into the station," Gold grumbled. "If you can't trust me with simple information, you certainly can't trust me with your life, which is exactly what we're doing out here together."

Stanton nodded. He'd accomplished his goal. It hadn't escaped his notice that Gold had said, 'You lied to me *too*,' thereby confirming her own lie.

He knew some of Gold's protest was just show to get him to stop pressing her. He also knew some of it was a genuine sense of betrayal. He knew it because he had felt it too when Lin explained that Gold had lied to him.

He was irritated that it bothered him so much. But he was glad to see it irritated her just as much, maybe more.

"All right," Stanton replied. "Let's go."

They made their way back up the emergency ladder and out onto the roof. Stanton poked his helmeted head down for one more look. No sign of Dekker's body, or how it came to be moved. No sign of the hull breech. At least they got the antibiotics.

The walk back was uneventful. He didn't try to talk to Gold because he knew she wouldn't talk back. They just walked past the ruins under the space station. The sun was starting to set and it would soon be pitch black and deathly cold.

When they reached the airlock, Stanton commed inside and Lin opened the doors for them.

"Welcome back," Lin said. "How did it go?"

Stanton disconnected his helmet with a whoosh, then lifted it off and looked at Gold. She did the same.

"We got the antibiotics," Gold announced as she extracted the pill bottle from her suit pouch.

Lin was visibly relieved. "Daniel, er, Commander Mtumbe will be glad to hear that," she said. Then she added, "He seems a little weak."

Before Stanton could do much more than nod, Rusakova came running in. "What of Nils's body?" she practically pleaded. "Were you able to move it?"

Stanton looked at Gold, and Gold at him. If Rusakova had moved the body, Stanton thought, she was doing a hell of an acting job.

"Nils's remains are fine, Oksana," Gold assured her. "The breech in the sickbay hull was big enough to totally replace the station air with Martian atmosphere. It's cold and dry. He'll be fine till we can give him a proper burial tomorrow. Isn't that right, Captain?"

Rusakova looked at Stanton, hope clear on her face. "Is that all true, Captain?"

Stanton looked into her eyes and just couldn't bring himself to tell her the truth. "Uh, sure. Yes. Yes, what Gold said."

Rusakova finally exhaled and managed a weak, but genuine smile. "Thank you," she said. "Thank you, Captain. And thank you, Agent Gold."

She walked off back toward the commissary.

Lin nodded to Stanton and Gold. "I'm glad you're back safely," she said, then she turned back to the control glass across the small room.

Gold leaned onto Stanton's shoulder and put her full lips right next to Stanton's ear, her soft blonde hair falling against his cheek.

"Now we're in a lie together, Johnny," she whispered.

Then she patted him on the butt and sauntered off toward the entry bay to return her suit.

41

Dinner was a quiet affair. Petrov ate in his room with Rusakova. Mtumbe took his antibiotics then ate in the commissary with Stanton and Lin. Gold said she wasn't hungry and wanted to lie down. By the time lights-out came around, everyone was glad for the opportunity to put the long, terrible day behind them.

As they readied themselves for lights out, Stanton pulled Mtumbe aside.

"I need your help with something tonight," he whispered. "How are you feeling?"

"Well enough," Mtumbe answered. "Probably a little more tired than I'd like, but that should go away now that I took my antibiotics. What do you need?"

Stanton looked around to make sure no one was eavesdropping, then he lowered his voice even more.

"We need to send word back to Command," he whispered, so low Mtumbe could barely hear it. "About Dekker's death, and about the damage to the station from the sandstorm."

Mtumbe nodded. "Agreed," he whispered back. "But why is it a secret?"

"Gold." Answered Stanton. "I don't want her to know we're going to do this."

"We?" joked Mtumbe. "Sounds like it's you who's doing this."

Stanton smiled. "Yeah, but you agreed to help, remember?"

Mtumbe nodded. "I should have known better. But why don't you want Gold to know? Do you really think she didn't comm back to Earth?"

"Well, she said she did," answered Stanton. "But I know she's lied to me before, so I can't necessarily believe she really did it."

"Fair enough," said Mtumbe. "So what's the plan? You want me to lock her in her cabin while you go comm Command?"

"Kind of the opposite," answered Stanton. "I'm going to go to her cabin and distract her while you sneak onto the ship and comm Earth."

"Distract, huh?" Mtumbe elbowed him lightly in the ribs. "Her cabin, huh? Sounds dangerous."

Stanton frowned. "Come on, Daniel, this is serious."

"Not that I blame you," Mtumbe went on. "She's a fine looking woman. A little cold, if you ask me, but I'm not a captain. She might be perfect First Mate material, if you know what I mean."

"Daniel?" Said Stanton.

"Yes, Captain?"

"Shut up," Stanton smiled. "And that's an order."

Mtumbe returned Stanton's smile. "Aye aye, Cap'n."

42

"Knock, knock," said Stanton as he rapped on the doorframe of Gold's cabin. The door was ajar a few inches. Enough for Stanton to see that Gold had stripped down to her bra and shortpants.

She turned to see Stanton, but didn't seem to care that she was in a state of undress. She also didn't say anything, but instead returned to what she was doing, namely pulling the sheet back to get into bed.

"Agent Gold?" Stanton pressed. "Do you have a moment?"

"For you, Captain?" she replied with a cold smile over her smooth shoulder. "Of course. Please enter my bed chamber."

The bed chamber comment sent Stanton's heart racing for a moment. Or if not racing, at least it picked up from a walk to a light jog.

"Thanks, Gold." He pushed the door open and walked in a few steps. "I thought maybe we should talk about what happened today."

Gold shrugged and sat on her bed. She let her thin, muscular arms hang between her knees. Stanton tried not to stare at how it accentuated her breasts. He was pretty sure he failed.

"So what happened today?" Gold asked. When Stanton didn't immediately reply, she added, "What happened that we need to talk about?"

"Well, the whole honesty and trust thing, I guess."

Gold nodded. "Yeah I figured that was it." She grimaced in thought. "I'm not sure we really need to talk about it. Seems pretty settled to me."

Stanton was surprised. "Settled?" he asked. "It seems totally unsettled to me. That's what we should talk about."

Gold shrugged and raised her palms. "Fine, if you want to be a girl about it."

This wasn't going at all like Stanton expected. He really couldn't figure her out. "A girl about it? What's that supposed to mean?"

"It means you want to talk about your feelings," Gold explained. "And you want everything 'out in the open' and 'on the table.'" She raised her fingers to make air quotes to emphasize the phrases. "And you just won't be able to 'move on' until we've said out loud all the things we're thinking inside."

Stanton thought for a moment. "That's not what I want."

Gold smiled. "It's not?"

"No," Stanton answered, "I just wanted to make sure we have an understanding, especially about Dekker."

"Good," said Gold. "I didn't want to have to stop liking you."

She smiled sideways at him, a smile both cold and inviting, approving and defiant, reassuring and challenging.

That sent his heart racing again, although in part because he remembered why he was really there and what he was really doing. How much would she hate him if she knew his real plan? Mtumbe hadn't made up his comments out of whole cloth. There was a reason he wanted to spend time and talk with Gold and it wasn't just to make sure she didn't interfere with Mtumbe's efforts to comm back to Command.

"Glad to hear it," he said. Not a perfect reply, but good enough. He wasn't in high school and this wasn't the cute girl from his homeroom class. Still, it kind of felt a little like that anyway.

Gold stared at him, but Stanton didn't say anything more, so she swung her hands together. "So," she emphasized the word with a quiet clap. "What's our understanding? You called this meeting, so I figure you've got something in mind."

"Uh, right," said Stanton. "Well, I figure we should make sure we're on the same page when it comes to Dekker's body."

"Agreed," said Gold. She leaned back against the wall and crossed her legs. She had really nice legs. "We told Rusakova that we moved the body to a safe location."

"I thought we told her it was safe inside the sick bay." Stanton countered.

"Right, right," agreed Gold. "I just meant that we moved it from sitting there on the examining table or something. But we did tell her the room was breeched and so it was the same as if we'd taken it outside. That's what I meant."

"So the body is still in sick bay, but we moved it to the

floor, maybe a corner? And covered it?"

"Right," said Gold.

"Of course we also said we'd do the burial tomorrow," Stanton pointed out. "I'm not sure how we do that without a body."

Gold smiled. "See, that's why it's good you came to talk to me. That problem goes away as long as you can think of a reason we can't get around to the funeral tomorrow."

"But he deserves a decent burial," Stanton protested.

Gold just stared at him for a moment. Then she shook her head slightly as she said, like a kindergarten teacher to the kid who eats paste, "We don't have a body, Captain. What are we going to bury?"

Stanton nodded and raised an index finger. "Ah. Good point."

He thought it over. "Then we'll need something else to explain the delay. I mean, we can't stall forever."

"We don't have to stall forever," Gold explained. "We just have to stall until we leave this godforsaken rock. What did you say that'd be, maybe a day or two before we can leave? So we stall until then, lament our inability to give him a proper burial, then salute his memory to Deimos, Phobos, and the stars."

Stanton was a bit taken aback. "Wow, I'm impressed. You've thought this all out, I see."

"Not really," Gold smiled. "I've been doing this since I was a kid. With parents like I had you learned how to lie and keep the lie alive. This is nothing."

Stanton wasn't sure what to say. He suddenly felt deeply ashamed that she had opened up to him even as he was essentially deceiving her. He just hoped it would end up being worth it.

He also wasn't sure whether he should ask what she meant by parents like she had. It wasn't the first time she had made a veiled reference to some trouble growing up. It seemed like an invitation to inquire, but he wasn't sure she really wanted that, or that he really wanted to know. That might be a one way road to some place he'd rather just know existed without having to take the full tour.

Still, he was flattered, and tempted, that she seemed to be opening just a crack for him at least to peer inside. He leaned forward to ask her.

And that's when Mtumbe came smashing into the room.

"Captain! Captain!"

He looked like hell. He was out of breath and sweat was beading on his forehead. Plus his eyes were red rimmed and he was obviously favoring his injured leg again.

Stanton's jaw dropped. What was Mtumbe doing? Didn't he know enough not to come find him while he was still talking to Gold?

"Uh, Daniel?" he said. "Kinda busy here."

Gold narrowed her eyes and looked at the two men.

Mtumbe either ignored or didn't understand Stanton's message. "It's the comm system on the ship, Captain."

Gold threw an icy stare at Stanton. "You bastard."

Oblivious, Mtumbe repeated, "The ship's comm system, Captain. It's totally destroyed!"

43

"You bastard," Gold repeated. "You lied to me. You tricked me."

"I talked with you," Stanton asserted. "We can talk about who's been lying to who if you want."

"Whom," said Gold.

Stanton shook his head. "What?"

"Who's been lying to whom," Gold corrected. "So you're a bastard with bad grammar."

Just then Rusakova came rushing in. She too was dressed for sleep. She grabbed Mtumbe. "Did you say the ship's comm equipment is destroyed?"

Lin walked up behind her, calmly, but listening intently. Petrov stood in the doorway of his cabin, close enough to hear.

"Yes," answered Mtumbe. "It doesn't work at all."

"Was it smashed?" Stanton asked.

"No," replied Mtumbe. "You wouldn't know from looking at it. All the controls are there, but it doesn't respond."

"Just like the station's comm equipment," observed Lin.

"That's what I thought too," explained Mtumbe, "so I opened up the control glass and looked inside. There was nothing there. All the comm hardware had been removed. Just like the equipment on the station's roof."

All eyes turned to Gold.

"What? You all think I did it?" she rolled her eyes. "That's idiotic. I don't need to do that. I am the ranking officer for communication issues. I just order you not to send comms and I get what I want. Why would I need to remove our ability to do it?"

Mtumbe shrugged and looked to Stanton. Gold looked at him too.

"Then again," she went on. "Maybe I'm wrong about that. Apparently Commander Mtumbe was trying to send a communication without my authorization. Did you know about that, Captain Stanton?"

Before Stanton could answer, Mtumbe stepped in. "No, ma'am. I went on my own. The captain didn't know anything about it."

Gold didn't seem convinced, but it didn't matter because Stanton raised his arms and spoke.

"Okay, enough. We've had enough lies and half-truths since we landed on Mars. It's time to lay everything on the table."

He shot a quick twinkling glance to Gold, who had to hold back a begrudging smile at his use of her cliché.

"So I'll start," Stanton went on. "Commander Mtumbe went to the ship at my request." He thought for a moment, then corrected himself. "At my order. To send a comm back to Command that Dekker was dead and the station was damaged. I asked him to do that because I wasn't convinced

Agent Gold had actually ever sent a communication and I hadn't seen her do so."

"I didn't lie about that, Captain," Gold protested. "I sent those comms."

Stanton shrugged. "Okay. But I know Agent Gold hasn't been completely honest with everyone."

The crew all looked at Gold, who crossed her arms defiantly. She glared at Stanton, but didn't say anything.

"I know," Stanton went on, "because I joined her in one of the lies."

He turned to face Rusakova directly. "Oksana, we lied when we told you Dekker's body was safe. It wasn't. In fact," he paused, unsure how to phrase it, "it's missing."

Rusakova cocked her head at the captain as her eyebrows knitted together. "Missing?" she asked. "How can that be?"

Stanton shrugged and shook his head. "I don't know. But that's the truth and I should have told you that when we got back from sick bay."

Petrov had made his way to stand silently behind the others.

"Well, where is his body?" Rusakova yelled. "Where is Nils's body?!"

"That's what I'm trying to explain," Stanton answered. "I don't know."

"I know," groaned Petrov.

44

Rusakova turned around and looked Petrov in the eye.

"Do not toy with me, Aleksandr," she warned. "I will not tolerate it."

"I do not toy with you, Oksana," Petrov replied earnestly. "I simply know where our friend's body has gone."

Oksana crossed her arms and narrowed her eyes. "Fine, then, Aleksandr. Where did his body go?"

Petrov's raised a calm eyebrow. "*Rusalka,*" he said simply.

"*Rusalka*?!" Rusakova repeated incredulously. "That's, that's... You are crazy, Aleksandr!"

"What's a *rusalka*?" Stanton asked.

"It's an old superstition," Rusakova growled. "It's supposed to be some sort of ghost."

"It is a well known traditional spirit," Petrov corrected. "A ghost who steals the bodies of the freshly departed to try to become mortal again."

"That's kinda creepy," Mtumbe observed from his spot leaning against the doorframe.

"It is kind of preposterous," Rusakova said. "And completely fabricated. In the days of grave robbers and body snatchers, when modern medicine was first developing, doctors needed fresh bodies to dissect and examine. Religious objections prevented families from donating bodies to science, so the only way to get a fresh body was to steal it. Then doctors, and the grave robbers who supplied them, made up the *rusalka* to trick people into thinking their loved one's body had been stolen by a malevolent spirit, instead of a criminal doctor."

Petrov smiled. "Skeptics always have an explanation, Oksana," he said, "but it is not as simple as that. There are reports of *rusalkas* from long before the first doctors snatched the bodies of condemned prisoners for scientific studies. From the time before even the first Christian missionaries, the people of rural Russia knew to bury their dead quickly before the *rusalkas* could steal them away."

He turned to the rest of the crew even as Rusakova's face reddened in anger.

"*Rusalkas* are the spirits of people who died to soon," Petrov went on. "They are not ready to pass on to heaven and so must walk the earth. Sometimes they try to steal bodies in the vain hope of entering the body and coming back to life"

"I hate you, Aleksandr Petrov," Rusakova snarled.

"I simply speak the truth," he answered, "which is more than your captain did for you."

Stanton felt the sting of that comment, but couldn't say it wasn't deserved. Nevertheless Gold stepped in to defend him.

"That was my lie," Gold asserted. "The captain was put in an awkward spot, so he went along with it until he could confront me on it. He thought it might go to communications and feared I outrank him on it. He waited until he got the chance to question me about it. That's what he was doing when you all barged in."

That was almost true, Stanton thought. He was impressed despite himself. She was very good at lying.

"All I mean to say," Petrov qualified, "is that my story explains what happened, while yours does not. Therefore my story is superior."

"I'm not sure that's the test, Petrov," Stanton said. "I think we could also agree that we simply don't know what happened, rather than having to resort to believing in ghosts."

"Especially ghosts on Mars," Lin finally said something. "Your explanation of *rusalkas* may make sense on Earth, but I daresay it makes no sense here on Mars."

"Oh, but it does," Petrov grinned almost maniacally. "That is the beauty of it. It not only explains what happened to Dekker, it explains what happened to the first crew as well."

"What are you talking about, Petrov?" Stanton was both angry and intrigued. He desperately wanted the answer to what had happened to the first crew, even if it was only so he could feel good about giving the order to go home.

Petrov's dark eyes smiled. "This station was built on some sort of Martian burial ground. Perhaps the last of the Martians were buried here. For some reason they have been unable to pass on to the next reality. They have waited billions of years with no hope of ever changing their fates. Then we arrive—or rather, the first crew arrives. As with us, the spirits cause little mishaps until one of the crew dies. Then another, then another. All in the hopes of getting a fresh body to try to inhabit and come back to life. It explains why Dekker's body is gone, and it explains why we have been unable to find even the bodies of the first crew."

Rusakova started to cry again and could only manage to mutter, "Oh, Aleksandr. Oh, Aleksandr."

Mtumbe looked at Gold, who declined to return the look, instead keeping her eyes fixed intently on Petrov.

"I'm sorry, Petrov," said Stanton, "but that makes no sense. There's no life on Mars."

Mtumbe raised his injured leg and coughed in contradiction.

"That could have been an Earthborne bacteria brought here on the ship," Stanton asserted. "That's probably why the antibiotics even worked."

"Yeah," said Mtumbe wiping his brow, "about that." Then he saw the look in Stanton's eye. "Never mind. I'll tell you later."

"And what's more," Stanton went on. "Even if there had been life on Mars, and even if it evolved into sentient life capable of building temples and stealing bodies, it makes no sense that they would try to steal human bodies."

Petrov didn't have to reply to that point. Lin beat him to it.

"Actually, Captain," she said, "that may the one strength of Lieutenant Petrov's theory."

Petrov smiled even as the rest of them looked at her in bewilderment.

"That is," she explained, "if you understand that humankind originally traveled to Earth from Mars."

45

Stanton was speechless. Gold kept her poker face. Rusakova fought back new sobs of disbelief.

Mtumbe smiled.

"What did you say?" asked Stanton, dumbfounded.

"There are people who believe that humans first came to Earth from Mars," Lin explained. "Perhaps because life was no longer possible on Mars, but in any event the theory is that they came to Earth and started over. It supposed to explain how humans just suddenly appear about ten thousand years ago."

"It doesn't explain why we have ninety nine percent the same DNA as chimps," Stanton shot back.

"Please don't misunderstand me," Lin responded politely. "I am not suggesting I believe this theory. I am simply pointing out that the theory exists and if it were true, then the spirits here would in fact be ancient humans more than willing and desirous of seizing a modern human body."

Petrov smiled broadly, displaying all of his teeth, even those in the far back of his mouth. "It explains much," he said.

"And much more than the lies we have been telling each other."

"So what happens now that your precious spirits know we have figured out who they are and what they are doing to us?" Rusakova shouted. "What happens now, Aleksandr?"

And a ghostly metallic wail echoed through the station.

"Do not make them angry, Oksana," said Petrov. "We will not like them when they are angry."

46

"It's just the ventilation system," assured Stanton. He almost believed it himself. "Which brings me back to what we were talking about. The ship's comm system."

Gold turned to Mtumbe. "Commander, can you describe exactly what was missing?"

"Not really," he answered. "That would require me knowing what was supposed to be there in the first place. My expertise is more engines and propulsion. I could look at a ion engine and tell if a part were missing, but I can't do that with comm electronics. Still, I can tell you that there wasn't anything left, so I guess what was missing was everything."

"Oh, why are we pursuing this charade?" Rusakova wailed. "Gold is a liar. She lied about Nils and she's lying about the comm system. She's the one who knows best how the equipment works. She's the one who dismantled it so no one could comm back to Command."

"That's not true," Gold replied firmly.

"Really?" screamed Rusakova. "Do you even know what truth is? Do you know what lies do to people?"

"Sometimes the lies do a lot less damage than the truths," Gold replied coldly.

"Okay, that's enough," Stanton felt obliged to step in. "This yelling won't settle anything. If Gold says she didn't do it, we should believe her."

"Thank you, Captain," said Gold.

"But we should also verify it," he went on.

He turned to Lin. "Lieutenant, did you manage to reactivate the station's video surveillance system?"

"What?" gasped Gold. "You didn't tell me you were reactivating that."

"It's not a communications issue," Stanton replied. "I tasked Lin with it and advised Mtumbe as second-in-command. There was no need to advise anyone else."

"You mean there was no need to alert anyone else," Gold spat, "so you could catch somebody doing something they shouldn't do."

"Or doing something they lied and said they didn't do," said Rusakova.

Gold sneered at her but didn't reply.

"So we can view the video of who entered the ship today?" Stanton confirmed with Lin.

"Yes, Captain," Lin replied. "We can watch the playback in the comm center."

"Then by all means, let's go," said Stanton. He smiled at Gold. "Ladies first."

Gold just shook her head at him. "What is it, the twentieth century?"

Stanton shrugged as Mtumbe, Lin, and the Russians started heading for the comm center.

"Just let me pull on some clothes," said Gold in a

normal tone. Then, after looking to make sure the others were out of earshot, she said to Stanton. "There's something I need to tell you."

Stanton shook his head. "Come on, Gold. No more lies, no more excuses."

"God, shut up, John," Gold said. "Stop with the righteous captain bit and come back to reality. There's something you need to know."

Gold's words and tone shook him. Especially the familiarity of calling him by his first name. He liked how it sounded when she said it.

After a moment he composed himself enough to ask, "What is it?"

Gold looked down the hallway again, then tapped the kit bag at the foot of her bed. In the lowest voice possible, she whispered, "Somebody stole my gun."

47

"You brought a gun?!" Stanton was beside himself. "Are you crazy?"

"Simple security," Gold defended.

"Not in outer space!" Stanton answered.

"Keep your voice down, Captain," Gold admonished with a finger to her lips and a glance down the hall after the others.

"Not in outer space," Stanton repeated in a near whisper. "One bullet could breech the hull of the station. Or worse yet, it could have breeched the hull of the ship."

Gold shook her head at him. "It's not a bomb, Captain. It isn't like it would have just gone off on its own."

"Not really my point," Stanton countered. "My point is that were not in the Arizona desert. We're in the Martian desert. A bullet through the wall of some adobe rambler means a little extra ventilation or a trip to the store for some spackle. Here extra ventilation means poisonous carbon dioxide and there is no hardware store to run to for some fucking spackle."

Gold crossed her arms. "I know all that. I didn't bring a gun just for fun, or even on my own initiative. I was instructed to do so at the highest levels."

Stanton was flabbergasted. "Why? Why would they put this mission in jeopardy like that?"

"This mission has been in jeopardy since the day Mars came out from behind the sun and we'd lost all contact with the colonists. There was no telling what happened. Hell, we've been here two days now and we don't even know what happened."

Stanton had to admit that point with a shrug and a curt nod.

"So when they sent a team of astronauts, of explorers, out to see what had happened, they needed to be open to the possibility of criminal activity or worse."

"Criminal activity?" Stanton repeated. "What are you talking about?"

"What if we had landed," Gold posited, "and it had turned out that half of the colonists had turned on the other half and we were faced with a hostile situation?"

"This isn't some apocalyptic video game," Stanton said.

"Neither is it some children's picture book about 'Mars: Our Friendly Red Neighbor,'" Gold reproved. "This is serious and we needed to be ready to defend ourselves."

Stanton could see her point, although he didn't agree it justified the dangers of having a firearm inside a space station on a planet with a poisonous atmosphere, let alone aboard a ship traveling through the vacuum of space.

"Fine," he said. "Let's assume that's all true. Why do you need it now and why didn't you tell me?"

"As to the last question," Gold replied, "I just told you.

As to the first, have you seen Petrov lately?"

"You're going to shoot Petrov?"

"Of course not," Gold spat. "Don't twist my words. You said you wanted open dialogue between us. That won't work if you don't hear what I'm saying. I learned a long time ago not to waste my time talking to someone who hears what they want to hear instead of what I'm actually saying."

Stanton took a deep breath. "Okay, I'm listening."

"Thank you," replied Gold. "Petrov is unstable. You yourself have put him under detention. As you well noted, there is no jail here. He has been compliant thus far. However, it may become necessary to use force to restrain him. To that extent having a firearm may be useful."

Stanton shook his head. "I see your point, but it actually illustrates mine. If you threaten to use a gun, you better be willing to use it. And if you use it, you could kill us all with a catastrophic hull breach."

"Depends on how good of a shot you are," Gold replied.

"Not necessarily," Stanton countered. "A through and through shot could pierce the wall behind them."

"A head shot usually doesn't exit the skull again."

Stanton just stared at her for several moments. "I see you've given this a lot of thought."

Gold smiled, the kind of smile a predator might allow itself after spotting its prey.

Then Mtumbe limped up to them, a little out of breath. "Hey guys, we need you in the comm center. There's a problem."

48

Stanton and Gold walked in to the comm center with Mtumbe right behind them. Lin was seated at the control glass. The monitor on the wall was activated and paused with a view of the entry bay airlock. Rusakova stood behind her. Petrov sat on the floor, knees pulled up, and chin resting on his forearms.

"Mtumbe said there's a problem?" Stanton asked Lin as he stepped over to the control glass. He looked up at the monitor. "Looks like it's working to me."

"Yes, I got it to work all right," Lin answered. "But here, watch this and you'll see the problem. I queued it up to right after you two got back from sick bay. It shows no activity until the time we sat down for dinner."

"Then what does it show?" asked Stanton.

"Watch for yourself," replied Lin and she pressed the play icon on the control glass.

They all watched as the camera showed the airlock, but no one ever passed by or entered it.

Finally Lin asked Stanton, "Did you see that?"

Stanton replied, "I'm not sure. I don't think I saw anything."

"Look again," said Lin. "Do you see that shadow there? Down in the bottom left corner?"

Stanton looked. "Yes."

"Okay, watch and tell me what happens to it," Lin instructed. She queued up the clip again and Stanton watched.

"Um... it looks like it's getting a little bit longer," he observed.

"Right," answered Lin. "As the sun moves west. Now watch it closely."

He watched and this time he noticed how suddenly the shadow was short again.

"Did you see that?" Lin asked excitedly.

"It jumped back to being short again."

"Exactly" said Lin.

"What does that mean?" Stanton asked.

"It means someone accessed the recording and doctored it," answered Lin, "replacing what really happened — someone entering the ship — with this loop of previous footage."

Stanton looked at the screen again.

"Whoever took out the comm equipment," Lin repeated, "Erased the evidence of entering the ship."

All eyes turned to Gold.

"Nice," she snarled. "Everything up till now has been the fault of some extraterrestrial gremlin—"

"Poltergeist," corrected Petrov from his seat on the floor.

"Thanks," Gold said sarcastically. "So everything up

until now has been caused by malicious spirits of ancient Mars, but now suddenly I'm the one who stole or comm equipment and doctored the surveillance tape?"

"It does make a certain sense," Stanton said. "You had to know we might try to comm back to Command behind your back."

"And you have the technical expertise to know how to manipulate digital media like the surveillance recording," added Rusakova.

"Plus the timing," pointed out Mtumbe. "It obviously happened during dinner, but you're the only one who didn't eat dinner with us. You claimed you weren't hungry and wanted to lie down."

"I didn't 'claim' anything," replied Gold. "I wasn't hungry and I did want to lie down."

She crossed her arms and surveyed the eyes against her.

"I do understand," she said calmly, "why you would suspect me. But before you condemn the outsider to burn at the stake, hear me out."

The reference to unfair judicial practices in remote, isolated colonies struck a chord inside Stanton. "Let her speak."

"Thank you," Gold said. "First, I'm not the only one who is tech-savvy enough to insert an image loop. That's pretty basic, right, Lin?"

Lin gave up an uncomfortable grin. "Er, yes," she agreed. "I could do it as well."

"Second," Gold went on, "the timing doesn't mean anything. Whoever did this could have placed two image loops: the real one and another one specifically to throw suspicion on me."

"Well, now, that's a little paranoid," Stanton said.

"Really?" Gold laughed. "You mean paranoid like everyone accusing me of something I didn't do?"

Stanton nodded. She had a point.

"Finally," Gold pressed. "I have no reason to do this. Quite the contrary. I can simply order you all not to send communications, and even the captain has to—or at least is supposed to—obey me. Besides, if I know enough how to remove the equipment, I certainly know how to password protect it. I can lock you all out without needing to remove hardware.

"In fact," she grinned, "I had already done that. So even if the equipment had been there, Mtumbe wouldn't have been able to send any comms."

The others looked at each other. Lin looked to the others and confirmed with a nod that such a password could definitely have been implemented.

"So really," Gold went on, "this is the worst possible situation for me. The one area I had control over is now removed. So now, not only am I an outsider, but I am completely irrelevant."

The rest of the crew looked at one another.

"She does have a point," Stanton said.

"Sounded pretty convincing to me," added Mtumbe.

"A little too convincing," said Rusakova. "Almost rehearsed."

"Oh, for God's sake," Gold threw her arms up. "Fine. I don't really care if you believe me. I know what the truth is. That will have to be enough."

It was time for Stanton to step in. "All right, we can get

to the bottom of this. Lin, can you examine the recording some more to try to figure it out."

"Yes, Captain," Lin replied simply.

"Good," Stanton said. "But don't stay up too late. You're not going to stay up two nights in a row. For the rest of us, it's time to get back to bed. I think we could all use the rest."

Everyone filed out of the comm center, even Petrov, and turned toward the sleeping berths. As Gold and Stanton reached the door, Gold grabbed his arm and whispered, "I didn't do it, John. You have to believe me."

Stanton grimaced as he thought of all the lies she had already told him. "Why should I?"

"Because," explained Gold, "it means someone else did."

49

Stanton walked Gold to her chamber and wished her a good night. He thought it looked like he was the captain walking a suspect to their holding cell. But he knew better. And so did she.

As he turned to leave, Gold whispered, "I know you believe me, John."

When he turned around again, he wasn't sure what to say.

But Gold was. "Whatever's happening, we're gonna have to deal with it eventually. You're gonna have to trust me."

"Then you're going to have to give me a good reason to. Good night, Gold."

But in the event, it wasn't a very good night. The strange, haunting metallic wail they'd heard earlier returned. It would start and echo through the ventilation, rising and falling and fading away before returning seconds or minutes later. That in turn led to half-audible rantings and cries by Petrov. On top of it all, Mtumbe spent the better part of the night moaning in a feverish sleep.

Stanton lay awake most of the night thinking. He should have been thinking about Mtumbe, the ship's communication system, the doctored video, Dekker's missing body, the Martian burial ground, Petrov's schizophrenic ravings, the fate of the first colonists—anything and everything other than what, or rather whom, he was thinking of.

By the time the Martian dawn arrived no one was any more rested than the night before. At least Lin had been productive.

"What did you find out?" Stanton asked her over his breakfast mush as she walked into the commissary.

She sat down across from him, and next to Rusakova who was eating quietly but raised her head in obvious interest as Lin sat down.

"I decided to go back to the beginning of the video footage," Lin explained, "so I would have some ability to compare the new footage with a known quantity."

"Makes sense," Stanton commented. "Did it shed any light on what might have happened to them?"

"Well, that's the interesting part," Lin said.

"It did then?" Rusakova asked.

"No. Not at all," Lin replied. "Which is what is so interesting. Everything is totally normal until about the nine month mark."

"When communications were blocked by the sun," remarked Stanton.

"Correct," Lin went on. "Then the recordings just stop."

"Stop?" asked Stanton. "Like no recording at all?"

Lin made an equivocal gesture with her hands. "Not

exactly. The date and time stamps continue to advance, but the images just enter into a perpetual loop, the same hour of so of video repeatedly looped."

"Is there anyone in the video?" Rusakova asked.

Lin shook her head. "No. The station is completely empty in all the videos. They just loop repeatedly until the day before our arrival, at which point the system turned off."

"So according to the video, the colonists just suddenly disappear without warning?" Stanton confirmed.

"Exactly," Lin answered. "But I'm not sure what that means."

Just then Gold walked in. She seemed to have slept fine, looking fully rested, with her full blonde hair pulled back in a thick ponytail.

"Good morning everyone," she practically sang. Then she saw Lin. "Oh, Mei-Zhu. Did your research exonerate or condemn me?"

Lin thought for a moment. "I would lean toward exonerate. There is something strange with the video."

"That loop thing has been going on for nine months," Stanton explained.

"And it's not just that," Lin said. "There are also images, very faint, but which do not appear to be looping."

Stanton's brow furrowed. "I'm not following you. What do you mean?"

"Well," Lin explained. "Even though the background images loop repeatedly, there are occasionally, well, I will call them figures, that pass through the environment. They are almost impossible to see. In fact I didn't even notice them at first, but then I noticed some anomalies in the pixels and focused in. There's something going on that was never properly recorded."

"Ghosts," said Petrov.

Everyone looked to the doorway where he was standing, glowering behind Lin.

"Isn't that what they are called?" he asked. "Those faint anomalies on the video recordings?"

Lin gave a reluctant nod to the rest of the group. "They are called that sometimes."

"Do you think you can get more information," Stanton asked Lin, "if you did some more examination?"

"I would expect so," Lin answered.

"Good," said Stanton. "Then here's the plan for today. Lin will continue to examine the video. Petrov and Rusakova will stay here while Gold, Mtumbe, and I go out and explore our alleged burial ground."

Lin frowned. "I am not sure that will work."

"Why not?" asked Stanton.

"Daniel, I mean Commander Mtumbe, does not feel well." Lin's face betrayed her concern. "I fear his infection has returned."

Stanton looked to Gold. She nodded her head toward the door.

"Go check on him," she said. "That's most important right now."

50

"Daniel?" Stanton knocked lightly on his friend's doorframe. The door was mostly closed. He pushed it open and was immediately met with a sour, musty smell. Not too strong, but unmistakable and unpleasant. He choked back a cough and stepped into the room.

It was dim, the only light coming from the hallway, but Stanton could see Mtumbe lying on the small cot, a rough blanket pulled up to his chin. He had his head turned to the wall, but rolled it back toward Stanton when he heard his voice.

"Hey, Captain," he said in a raspy tone. "What brings you to my humble abode?"

Stanton leaned against the wall opposite him. There wasn't really room to sit anywhere.

"I heard you weren't feeling too well."

"I think I've got a cold," Mtumbe joked from his pillow.

"I'll see if there's any chicken soup in the commissary," Stanton joked back.

Then, after a moment, Stanton asked, "The infection back?"

Mtumbe nodded. "Yeah, that has to be it."

"How's the leg?"

Mtumbe offered up a dark laugh. "Check for yourself."

Stanton reached over and lifted the blanket. The rancid smell he'd detected when he first walked exploded out from under the blanket, almost overwhelming him. The wound was active again, oozing a thin, foul smelling liquid, yellow in color, which left the skin shiny and pungent. The opening of the wound seemed to be mostly closed—at least there wasn't any red showing—but clearly the infection had returned.

"I've seen worse," said Stanton.

"You're a terrible liar," Mtumbe told him.

"Maybe I should get Gold in here," Stanton joked.

Mtumbe started to laugh but then caught himself. "It hurts to laugh," he explained. "But as far as Gold goes, she may be a liar, but I trust her too. She's not going to turn on us."

Stanton didn't really want to talk about Gold just then.

"Does it hurt much?" he asked instead.

"My leg? No, not really. It stinks, but it doesn't really hurt. Mostly it's just numb."

He took a deep breath. "It's the fever, headache, and shortness of breath I can do without."

"Did you take your antibiotic?" Stanton asked, seeing the bottle on the small shelf next to the bed. Lying behind it was the small Martian figurine Mtumbe had found under Lin's cot.

"Yeah," Mtumbe smiled. "Last night and this morning. Doesn't feel like it's working any more."

Stanton picked up the bottle and read it. Floxacilin. The

latest in generations of drugs descended from the original penicillin. Worked wonders on Earth. Not so much on Mars apparently.

"Well, keep taking it," Stanton advised unhelpfully. "Probably just a little relapse. Your body will fight it off soon enough."

"I'm sure you're right," Mtumbe coughed. "I just need some rest."

"Too bad, though," Stanton said, covering up the nasty leg again. "I was gonna take you sightseeing with me and Gold."

"Oh, yeah?" Mtumbe smiled. "Valles Marineris?"

"No, nothing as nice as that," Stanton laughed. "Closer to home. We're going to check out the stones under the station."

"Ah, our very own Martian burial ground."

"Exactly. It's always the tourist sights in your own backyard that you never get around to seeing."

Mtumbe smiled and nodded. Then he shivered a bit a pulled his blanket tighter.

"Hey, Captain?" he said. Then, breaking protocol, "John?"

"Yes, Daniel?"

"That Martian burial ground?"

"Yes?"

Mtumbe frowned. "See if they've got room for me. I don't think I'll be heading back with you guys."

Stanton was shaken. "Nonsense," he said. "Don't talk like that. Your white cells just need a little more time to figure out how to kick some Martian bacteria ass. You'll be back on your feet in no time."

Mtumbe smiled. "I'm sure you're right," he lied.

Stanton didn't believe it either.

51

"Change of plan," Stanton announced as he walked back into the commissary. "Mtumbe's in no shape to go anywhere. In fact he needs someone to look after him."

"I can do it," Lin volunteered.

"No, Lieutenant," Stanton answered. "Although I'm sure you would be his first choice, I need you to keep examining those tapes. I think they may be the key to figure out what is going on here."

Lin's shoulders drooped, but she understood why the captain felt as he did.

"That means I need you to do it, Oksana," Stanton said to the Russian woman.

Rusakova nodded. "Of course, Captain. But who will watch Aleksandr?"

Stanton smiled. "Agent Gold and I will. He's coming with us."

Gold looked up from her breakfast, but instead of protesting, she shook her head, smiled, and went back to eating.

It was Petrov who voiced concerns. "I am not sure I am in any condition to serve you properly," he said.

"I don't expect so either," Stanton said. "But I need to keep an eye on you."

Then Stanton walked over to the Russian. "Besides, Aleksandr. And I mean this sincerely, if you really can speak to the spirit world, then I may well need your talents. That is, if this is in fact a burial ground."

Petrov nodded. "Oh, it is, Captain. The only question is whether we end up buried there as well."

52

"This is a bad idea."

Petrov's voice echoed through the comm link into Stanton's and Gold's helmets. His accent and his disassociative demeanor rendered the voice even more distant and disturbing. It was haunting enough that Stanton couldn't stop himself from responding, "Shut up, Petrov."

"He's probably right," Gold piped in. "I'm not sure why we have to do this. At least right now."

"As far as timing, I don't think we'll get a later," Stanton answered. "As far as doing it at all, or why we're doing it, whatever were on top of is related to what we saw out there with Dekker. It may well shed light on what happened to the first crew. And if it also sheds some light on Dekker's death, that's even better."

"Don't forget the whole Ancient Martian Civilization thing," Gold reminded him.

Stanton looked down at the stone filled pit uncovered by the sandstorm. Large, smoothly cut rectangular stones lay perfectly parallel to each other. "I don't think I could forget that even if I wanted to."

Petrov leaned forward and gazed at the sight. Stanton and Gold watched him. Stanton wasn't ready to completely dismiss his 'abilities' as the ravings of a mad man. When he'd decided to bring Petrov along it wasn't simply to watch him so Rusakova could attend to Mtumbe. It was also to see if he might have some insight, some sixth sense observation that could help them. And more specifically, might help Mtumbe. Because although Stanton wasn't sure whether or not ghosts existed, he felt very confident that Mtumbe would soon be one if they didn't figure something out quick.

Gold seemed willing to trust his lead on it. He hadn't told her explicitly what he was thinking. He wasn't even sure he would have been able to. But he felt that Gold understood and although she might not have agreed, she was willing to follow. And help.

"I guess we'd better head down and examine those stones or something," Stanton said.

"Nothing like a clear order to inspire confidence," Gold joked.

But before he could reply, Petrov said, without opening his eyes, "Wait. I sense something here. Something evil. Something ..." he searched for the word, "sad."

Gold looked at Stanton and raised an eyebrow.

"Something evil and sad?" Stanton asked.

"No," Petrov answered. "Or rather, not exactly. There is evil here. And there is sadness. But they are not together. There are in conflict. I can not explain it more than that."

"Any voices, Aleksandr?" Gold asked.

Petrov shook his head. "None. Only feelings. Ideas. Emotions. They are strong despite the age of the place."

"Do you sense anything dangerous?" Stanton asked. "At least dangerous to us?"

Petrov was silent for a few moments as he considered what he was feeling. "I sense something unfortunate. But it is distant. Like the end of a movie that you can guess at when the film is only half over."

"Yeah, I hate movies like that," said Gold.

Stanton looked at her disapprovingly. "Not helping," he said. She shrugged and offered a pretty smile.

Stanton turned his attention back to the Russian. "Any reason we can't go see these things up close?"

Petrov breathed deeply. "Yes, I'm sure there is," he said. "But I cannot say why. So we might as well go."

"That's a hell of a pep talk, Petrov," said Gold. Then she turned sideways to the pit and started down sideways. After a couple of steps, she looked up at her companions. "Come on, boys. Try to keep up."

53

"After you, Captain," Petrov motioned toward Gold.

Stanton shook his head behind his faceplate. "I don't think so, Aleksandr. I'm supposed to be watching you. I don't want you tempted to stay up there without us. Especially since you're our canary in the psychic coal mine."

"I beg your pardon?" asked Petrov.

"Canary in a coal mine," Stanton repeated. "Miners used to take canaries down into the coal mines with them because if poisonous gasses seeped into the mine they would overwhelm the canary first."

"I understand the reference," Petrov answered. "There were mines in Russia as well. I was referring to using me as the one who dies first."

"Oh, that," Stanton laughed. "I just meant that if there are any negative spirits or energies, you will feel them, whereas Gold and I probably won't."

Petrov stared at him.

"Come on, Petrov," Gold called out from halfway down the incline. "It's okay to be a canary, but don't be a chicken."

Petrov looked at her with narrowed eyes. "I understand that reference as well," he said.

"Oh, good," she answered. "I'd hate for you two to get to stall even more without following me down here. I can tell you one thing—and I know you'll believe me—if you guys don't come down and I see something really cool? I ain't telling you."

"Well, I do believe that," Stanton said. Then he turned to Petrov. "Come on, Petrov, you go and I'll follow you down."

Petrov still hesitated.

Stanton sighed. "That's an order," he added finally.

Petrov sighed as well, then shrugged and started down into the pit, sideways like Gold. Stanton followed right behind, wondering what awaited them.

He didn't have to wait long.

"Captain," called Gold standing by one of the carved stones. It was on its side, but was nearly a meter thick and extended more than two meters in length. "Come look at this one."

Stanton stepped over to Gold and Petrov followed loosely behind, although while Stanton was looking directly at the stone, Petrov was looking up, down, and all around.

"What is it?" Stanton asked Gold as he reached her.

"Look at the scuff marks on the side here," said Gold. "And how sharp the edge is."

Stanton examined the stone carefully. "You're right."

Gold exhaled impatiently. "Of course I'm right," she said. "I'm not asking you to confirm my observations. I'm pointing them out because of what they suggest."

"Right," said Stanton quickly. "I knew that."

Gold waited a minute. "You don't know what they

suggest, do you?"

"I'm an astronaut," said Stanton, "not an archaeologist."

"Well, that's kind of my point," answered Gold. "I'm not an archaeologist either, but I've taken a few related courses, and one of the real basic ideas is that things wear down over time. But these have sharps edges and still bear the chisel marks from whatever carved them."

"So they're not a million years old?" Stanton deduced.

"Not even ten thousand years old like Lin suggested," Gold answered.

"Don't be so sure," Petrov warned. "The air here is very thin and there is almost no water, not even water vapor in the air. Water is one of the most powerful forces of wearing down. Things will not wear and age here like they do on water-rich Earth."

Gold didn't respond right away, which let everyone know she thought Petrov had a point. "Well, it's something to consider," she insisted.

Stanton offered his agreement and they spread out again to examine the exposed stones. Each was parallel to the others and in the same prone, extended position. After a few minutes, Stanton had worked his way to one side of them, Gold to the other and Petrov was wandering around between the two middle stones.

"I wish I knew what we were looking for," admitted Stanton over his comm link.

"We'll know it when we see it," assured Gold.

"Oh, I am seeing it," reported Petrov, "and I know it. Come see."

54

"What is it?" Stanton called over the comm link as he hurried toward Petrov's location. He couldn't move very fast in the bulky spacesuit. Gold made her way toward Petrov too, although she neither inquired nor hurried.

"I would prefer you see it yourselves and confirm or dispel my suspicions, Captain," Petrov answered, "rather than hazard a guess."

When Stanton arrived, Petrov pointed to what he'd found. Gold stepped up behind and saw it too. It was a crack in the ground, between two flat stones they had previously overlooked. The crack wasn't all that interesting. What was interesting was what was visible through the crack.

Nothing.

Not sand or dirt or rocks, but a big, black, unlit nothing.

"It looks like some sort of opening," Stanton opined.

"To a cavity, perhaps," Gold added.

"Or a chamber," Petrov suggested.

They all three bent down and started sweeping away

the sand and dirt. Soon they had exposed a large flat stone, one and a half meters wide and two meters long and about five centimeters thick. The gap they had first seen was visible over a portion of the front and one side, but otherwise it was flush against the sand.

"It's certainly big enough to be an entryway into somewhere," Stanton observed. "Do you think we can move this stone aside?"

"There's one way to find out," said Gold and she shoved her gloved fingers into the opening on the side. Stanton and Petrov followed suit into the groove at the front and they all shoved the stone diagonally away from where they had amassed.

It budged enough at the first shove to give them hope of moving it even as it settled back into place.

"Try spinning it," suggested Gold, "like the lid of a jar."

Stanton agreed and Petrov did as he was told. In a short minute they had managed to slide the stone enough to open up triangular openings at each corner.

"Now we can lift it," said Gold.

Stanton was thankful for the relative weakness of Martian gravity. Everything weighed considerably less than it would have on Earth. So although their muscles had weakened a bit after six months in zero gravity, it was a net gain in strength. They each reached under the large, thin slab and grabbed a hold of it.

"On three," said Stanton. "We lift it and move it to the other side of the opening, toward the station."

Gold and Petrov indicated their understanding and they all firmed their grips.

"One ... two ... three!"

They stone was lifted up and away, revealing not just an opening, but a chamber, with rudimentary, worn steps leading down into the blackness below.

Stanton pressed a button on his helmet. "Lin?"

It took a moment but the lieutenant answered, "Yes, Captain?"

"We've found something," reported Stanton. "We're going in."

"'In,' sir?"

"Yes, Lieutenant, in." Stanton turned on the powerful flashlight attached to the side of his helmet. "We may lose the comm feed."

"Uh, understood, sir," said Lin. Stanton could tell she wanted to ask for more information, but had decided against it.

Gold and Petrov activated their own helmet lights and they began a careful descent into the darkened chamber.

"I'll go first this time," Stanton said.

"Your turn to be the canary, I think," said Petrov.

"I'm not sure what we'll find, crew," he said, "but please alert me if you see or sense anything concerning."

"We're walking into a pitch black Martian catacomb," Gold observed. "Do you mean something more concerning than that?"

"Exactly," replied Stanton without missing a beat. "Use that as your baseline."

They reached the bottom of the mottled stairs and surveyed the room. It was a sort of antechamber, with a hallway extending away into the dark.

"Those Martians must have been pretty short," Gold said as their helmets nearly brushed the low ceiling.

"Or lazy," countered Stanton. "They didn't want to carve out more than they had to."

"I do not think we should disparage them," Petrov warned.

Stanton and Gold looked at each other and shrugged.

"Doesn't that way lead directly under the station?" Gold asked, changing the topic. She pointed a gloved hand into the recessed blackness.

"Exactly," replied Stanton. "About thirty meters and we'll be directly under the entry bay."

"Where I first saw the ghost," recalled Petrov.

Stanton decided not to argue with him. There was enough to worry about. He turned and shone his light on the wall to their left. It was the same dark red rock as the stones and chamber lid above. And like the stones it was marked with the scratches and scrapes of a carving tool.

"Do you think this room is carved from solid rock?" Gold asked. "That would have taken forever with hand tools."

Stanton inspected the wall more closely. "The only other explanation would be some sort of paneling to make it look that way. "Maybe if we look for a seam..."

But his thoughts were interrupted by the haunting, frightened voice of Petrov. "They're here."

"Who?" asked Stanton. "Who's here?"

"The spirits," answered Petrov. "I can feel them. They're here. The same ones I felt inside the station."

Gold looked to Stanton, who looked back blankly, uncertain what to say.

So Gold tried, "Are they saying anything?"

"It is not exactly speaking," Petrov answered. "It is more like a feeling they are trying to communicate."

Gold sighed. "Okay, well, what's the feeling? What are they telling us?"

Petrov turned to his compatriots with red rimmed, haunted eyes.

"Flee."

55

"Flee?" repeated Gold incredulously.

"That is what I feel," answered Petrov.

"Tell them, 'Not yet,' Petrov," instructed Stanton. "We need to check this place out first."

He pointed his suitlight down the hallway, but it was swallowed by the blackness.

"Tell them we're not afraid of them, too," added Gold.

"Speak for yourself," replied Petrov. "But in any event I do not feel malice from them just now. Simply a warning that we should flee this place."

"This place?" asked Gold. "You mean this chamber, or the whole damn planet?"

Petrov shrugged in the darkness. "Take your pick."

"Come along, you two," said Stanton, who was already several meters ahead. "There's more to see here."

Once they had caught up with him, Stanton flashed his light on the walls surrounding them. "We've reached an intersection of sorts," he advised. "To the left is an even smaller passageway, to our right is this hole."

Gold and Petrov looked to where the captain was pointing and sure enough there was a small irregularly shaped hole, less than half a meter in diameter, in the wall at about eye level.

"What's through the hole?" Gold asked.

"I can't quite tell," Stanton answered. "My light doesn't line up quite right. I'll shine my light through the hole and you look in, okay?"

Gold hesitated. "Why don't we have our canary stick his easily broken, glass plated face against the hole?" she asked, only half joking.

"I am a canary," Petrov answered, "not a guinea pig."

"Fine," answered Gold. "But this better be worth it."

She placed her gloved hands against the wall and leaned forward, leaving enough space for Stanton to twist his body and shine his light through. She peered inside.

"It looks like a crawl space," she reported. "I see one of the station's steel support beams and a small cavity with nothing but dirt and dust."

"The station must be directly above us," Stanton concluded.

"Were the support beams not driven into the ground by remotely controlled construction robots?" asked Petrov. "Before even the first colonists arrived?"

"Exactly," answered Stanton. "That support beam must have passed through an air pocket and cracked the wall to this vault."

"Thereby awakening the ancient Martian spirits who want to kill us," observed Gold dryly. "Great. Can we go now?"

"What about this other passageway?" Stanton asked.

Gold examined it critically. "We can't fit down there," she said. "Not without getting on our hands and knees."

Stanton had to agree with her. It was only half the height of the small hallway they were already in. Still, they had come this far.

"What do you think, Petrov?" he asked.

Petrov stared into the small passageway. "I think you have talked me into coming this far," he answered, "but you will not talk me into going down that passageway. Whatever I feel, I feel it most strongly from in there."

Stanton weighed his options. He wasn't about to ask one of the others to crawl down some unknown, haunted Martian catacomb. That left him two options: do it himself, or never find out what lay beyond. As bad as the first option seemed, the second was unacceptable.

You'll never be a true pioneer, Junior, he remembered Ferguson saying once, *if you're afraid of being the first to die.*

"Okay, then." Stanton bent onto hands and knees. "I'll go."

"Are you sure this is a good idea?" Gold asked. The suits weren't designed for wear and tear on the knee joints from crawling like a baby.

"No," Stanton answered, "but I'm doing it anyway."

The suits also weren't designed to have someone bend over and then tip his head back up to look forward. As a result, when the captain raised his face to look ahead, part of his view was blocked by the top of the helmet. In addition, the helmet light was in a fixed position, so it shone straight down, Stanton would have to rely on the light reflecting off the stone to illuminate whatever was ahead of him.

"Here goes," he said and started into the claustrophobic

passageway.

The floor and walls were simple dirt this far back, not the stone from the main passageway. He imagined the room smelled dank, like a wine cellar, but his helmet of course prevented any air from reaching his nostrils to confirm his suspicions. He found himself wondering absently whether the dank smell of Earthly caverns didn't originate from the dense moisture in the soil, and whether that would result in there being an entirely different, or even lack of, smell in a Martian cavern.

These thoughts distracted him enough that he almost overlooked the carving on the wall next to him as he got a few meters inside.

It was difficult to make out in the reflected helmet light, but it was definitely not just tool scrapes. It was an X. And above the X was what looked rather remarkably like a horse, or some similar four legged beast.

Stanton stared at it in wonderment and damned himself for not having activated his digital image recorder before crawling into the confined space. He couldn't reach the controls on the back side of his spacesuit belt. Maybe if he backed out again, he thought.

And that's when he noticed it, again barely lit in the dim reflected light from the downward facing helmet light. He crawled a few more steps until he was literally on top of it, his light shining directly on it and his face directly above it.

It was a figurine, just like the one Mtumbe had found inside the Station.

Stanton picked it up in his gloved hand and quickly, but carefully backed out of the passageway. He knew there was more to explore, including what looked like small, dark openings in the far wall, but he wanted to show the others what he had found, and he wanted to turn on his camera.

"What is it?" Gold asked as he suddenly crawled backwards out of the passageway. "Is everything okay?"

Stanton stood up and displayed the figurine for them.

"I found this."

Gold looked at it and shrugged. "What is it?"

But Petrov didn't ask what it was. He started backing away from it.

"It's okay, Petrov," Stanton said, but the Russian paid him no heed. Instead, he backed farther way, then turned and started running back toward the surface.

"Aw, shit," said Stanton and he ran after him, although a bit slower and considerably safer. The suits weren't meant for racing. Gold hurried behind and they caught up to Petrov just outside the entrance, where he was sliding in the loose Martian sand as he tried to climb up out of the depression that had uncovered the catacomb.

"Petrov, wait!" Stanton yelled over the comm link.

Then Lin broke in over the comm feed. "Captain, is that you?"

"Lin?" he responded.

"Captain, you have to come back inside right away." She sounded panicked. Lin never panicked.

"What it is?" Stanton asked

He looked at Gold, but she could only shrug in return.

"It's Daniel, Captain," Lin's voice cracked. "I think he's dying."

56

Stanton rushed through the airlock and down the hall toward the crew's cabins. Gold hurried herself equally but turned toward the ship. Petrov just dropped into a corner and curled into a ball, not even bothering to disconnect his helmet.

Rusakova had operated the airlock, but followed Stanton to Mtumbe's room, leaving Petrov alone.

Lin was standing at Mtumbe's head. His forehead was covered in a clammy sweat, his lips were dry and cracked, and his mouth hung open with only the shallowest of breathing.

The smell that was emanating from his leg was almost overpowering. If it hadn't been for the fact that Mtumbe was a friend and colleague, Stanton almost wouldn't have been able to stomach it.

"How are you doing, Daniel?" Stanton asked, but Mtumbe didn't respond.

"I think he can hear you," Lin said, "but he hasn't been responsive for the last thirty minutes or so."

"Hang on, Daniel," Stanton said. "You can beat this."

Just then Gold rushed in. It was noteworthy for two

reasons. First, Gold rarely rushed anywhere; it wasn't her style. Second she was carrying an injector.

"Here you go, Captain," she said as she handed it to Stanton. "This was my personal stash of antibiotics."

Stanton took the injector and shook his head. "Were you planning on killing all of us?"

"Planning?" Gold replied. "No. Prepared to? Yes."

Stanton wasn't as shocked as he thought he should be. But then he remembered his surroundings, and his task. He jabbed the injector of antibiotics directly into Mtumbe's neck and emptied the capsule. Mtumbe convulsed at the injection, but then laid back, unresponsive.

Stanton picked up the antibiotics pill bottle and opened it. He sniffed inside.

"These don't smell right," he said. "Not like other antibiotics I've taken. Gold, are you sure these are the right pills?"

"It was the only bottle in there marked as antibiotics, and it looked like the same bottle he'd been taking them from," she answered. "I'm not a chemist so I can't say whether they expired or something."

Stanton shook his head. "Well, they sure stopped working. Maybe the bacteria became resistant faster than the antibiotics could kill it."

"If so," said Lin, "then maybe Gold's antibiotic can kill off what's left before—"

But she couldn't finish the sentence. There was nothing left to do but wait and hope and pray.

Then Petrov walked in.

He had become quite the disturbing character since they'd arrived and Stanton knew no one wanted to deal with his foolishness while one of their own lay at death's door. Petrov seemed to sense it as well and said nothing. Instead, he stepped past Gold and Rusakova and over to the captain. Without saying anything he reached into Stanton's suit pouch and extracted the figurine. Stanton watched but didn't try to stop him or say anything. Next, Petrov took the matching figurine from the shelf over Mtumbe's bed. Then, still without saying a word, he left.

Rusakova backed out of the room next. Lin knelt down and started stroking Mtumbe's hair. Gold put a hand on Stanton's shoulder.

"Come on, John," she said. "Mei-Zhu will watch over him. Let's leave him to rest."

Stanton lowered his head but after a moment acquiesced to the suggestion. He squeezed Mtumbe's hand and whispered, "Get better, Daniel. That's an order."

Then he nodded a thank you to Lin and let Gold lead him out of the room and back to her cabin. He plopped down on the bed and put his head in his hands. He wasn't crying but he was tired.

Gold hesitated, then sat down next to him and put her arm over his shoulder.

"He was a good man, Cassie," Stanton rasped.

"He still is, John," Gold replied. "Don't give up hope just yet."

Outside, the sun started its early descent into the Martian dusk.

57

Dinner was quiet again. Lin stayed with Mtumbe while Stanton and Rusakova ate in the commissary. Gold was tasked with watching Petrov who had retreated to his cabin with the figurines. When Stanton had finished his meal, he went to relieve Gold so she could get something to eat. Rusakova had made it clear she couldn't deal with Petrov any more. Stanton suspected she didn't like being tied to him by their shared nationality.

In any event, Stanton crossed the hall and entered Petrov's cabin-turned-cell.

"I can take over now," he said to Gold, "if you want to get something to eat."

Gold stood up from the small stool by the door. "Thanks. He's been pretty docile. In fact, he hasn't said a word."

"I don't think he's said a word since we got back inside the station," Stanton remarked.

They both looked at Petrov. He was sitting on his bed, his legs pulled up under him cross legged, and was staring at the figurines he held, one in each hand.

"What's he doing?" Stanton whispered.

"I have no idea," Gold replied. "And I'm pretty sure I don't care either."

She slapped Stanton on the back. "Good luck with Rasputin." Then she headed to the commissary for dinner.

Stanton sat on the chair and watched Petrov for a few moments. He suddenly wished he'd brought something to read. Petrov just stared at the figurines, his head rolling ever so slightly to one side and back as he switched his focus from one statuette to the other. He appeared to have finally severed all ties with reality.

So Stanton nearly jumped off the stool when Petrov spoke.

"Objects have powers, you know, Captain," he said without looking up.

Stanton didn't reply. He figured Petrov would elaborate. He was right.

"They're called *goshons* in Russian. All other cultures have them too. Totems, tikis, voodoo dolls. They can hold spirits, both good and evil."

"Is that what you think happened to Mtumbe?" Stanton asked, trying unsuccessfully to mask his irritation at the suggestion. "You think he was attacked by an evil spirit from a wiki tiki doll?"

Petrov smiled but kept staring at his figurines. He held one of them up slightly. "When did this get into Commander Mtumbe's room?"

Stanton didn't really want to go down this road, but he went ahead and answered, "Yesterday."

"And how had he been doing before that?"

"He was starting to feel better."

"How has he fared since then?"

Stanton nodded. "He's gotten worse."

Petrov smiled again, not a smile at the misfortune of his crewmate, but rather a grimace of sickening understanding.

"Where did it come from?" he asked.

"Mtumbe found it hidden in Lin's room."

"Which means who found it originally?"

"Someone from the first crew."

"And where are they all now?"

Stanton grimaced. "They're dead."

Petrov shrugged.

Stanton needed one more question answered. "Then why are you still okay, Aleksandr? You have both *goshons*, right there in your hands."

Petrov nodded. Then he looked up for the first time to face his guest. "That is the very question I am pondering, Captain. I do not know the answer except to say that there are those who are immune to certain effects. Perhaps the spirits have no power over me, or perhaps they are choosing not to affect me."

"Or perhaps they just haven't started attacking you yet," Stanton suggested darkly.

Petrov smiled and nodded some more. Then he looked down again at his figurines. "That is the most likely explanation, I agree. And the one I am most hoping is true."

Petrov never ceased to surprise Stanton. He cocked his head at the Russian. "Now why would that be, Aleksandr?"

"Because the spirits of the *goshon* can only attack one person at a time," Petrov replied calmly. "If they begin to attack me it will mean they have ceased to attack Daniel. I can only hope it will not be because he has died."

"I hope that too," Stanton replied. "But I'd like to get us out of this without anyone else dying."

Petrov returned his gaze to the figurines in his grasp. "I have been shown shadows of my fate, Captain," he said as simply as telling the color of the sky. "I shall not be returning to Earth."

58

"Do not talk like that, Aleksandr." It was Rusakova. She had walked up behind Stanton in time to hear Petrov's last comment. "We will all be going home soon. Even Daniel."

Petrov smiled, but didn't look at her. "Oh, Oksana," he said. "I did not know you cared."

"I do not, Aleksandr," Oksana replied. "Not after all of the things you have done and said. But the captain is doing his best and does not need a self pitying, fake psychic stealing valuable time and energy from him."

Petrov frowned. "I am not self pitying," he protested. "And I am not a fake. I do not wish to be sensing the things I am sensing. I did not wish this for myself, Oksana."

"I am not so sure, Aleksandr. You have become very important, more important than you deserve. I wonder if this is not all some act just to be interesting."

"All right you two," Stanton interrupted. "I don't need another fight on board this station. What brings you to Petrov's cabin, Lieutenant?"

"Ah, yes," said Rusakova. "Gold said she needs to

speak with you. She asked me to watch Aleksandr for you so that you and she might talk."

Stanton mentally rolled his eyes. As if he didn't have enough to worry about.

"She said it was important."

"I'm sure she did." Stanton stood up from the stool. "You two play nice, okay?"

"Yes, Captain," said Petrov. "We will."

"I will try," was all Rusakova could promise.

Stanton stepped across the hall to the commissary where Gold was waiting for him.

"You beckoned, milady?" Stanton said as he sat down opposite her at the small table.

Gold acknowledged the joke with the faintest of smiles. "We need to talk," she said matter-of-factly.

"About what exactly?" There was so much that had happened since they'd arrived.

"What did you see in that passageway?" asked Gold. "Was it just the figurine?"

Stanton's first impulse was to lie and tell her 'Yes,' but he realized they would need to help each other. Besides, although he didn't exactly trust her, he had grown to respect her. Perhaps she might be able to make some sense out of what he'd seen.

"No, it wasn't just the figurine," he confided. "The passage went back quite a ways, into some even smaller recessed areas, barely big enough to fit in at all."

Gold didn't say anything, but her eyes encouraged him to go on.

"But what was most interesting," he said, "aside from maybe the figurine, was a carving in the wall."

Gold raised an interested eyebrow. "A carving? You mean like the tool marks we saw outside?"

Stanton shook his head. "No, it was more than that. It was an image."

"An image?" asked Gold. "Like a picture?"

"Maybe symbol is a better word," said Stanton. He pulled a plate over between them and grabbed a condiment packet. He tore the corner and squeezed out a line on the plate.

"It was an X," he explained as he replicated the image, "with something above it. I thought it looked like a horse, but it wasn't a very good drawing."

"So now you're an art critic?" joked Gold.

"More like a haunted Martian catacomb etching critic," replied Stanton with a grin. "I believe I'm mankind's foremost expert on the subject right now."

"I suppose that's probably true," Gold admitted.

Stanton finished drawing the horse-thing and moved his hands away in a 'ta da' motion.

Gold looked at it with curiosity, then looked again with recognition. She suddenly reached out and spun the plate so the image was right side up for her.

After a moment she said, "Oh, dear." She examined the sketch again. "John, we have to talk."

Stanton was surprised by the urgency underlying her tone.

"Don't tell me you drew it?" he tried joking.

"No, I didn't draw it," Gold said. "And I didn't carve 'Croatoan' in the corridor support post."

Stanton nodded. "I kind of already knew that, but thanks for confirming it."

Gold shook her head and exhaled in clear irritation. "They're related, John."

"Who are?" Stanton was confused.

Gold exhaled again. "The drawing you saw and the 'Croatoan' carving."

"You know, I do want to hear about that," Stanton interrupted, "but since you've finally admitted doing something you insisted you didn't do—or rather admitted to not doing something you insisted you did do—could you just explain to me why you said you did it?"

Gold shook her head. "Well, it was obvious no one from our crew had done it. And it was obvious that it was freaking everybody out. You were ready to comm back to Command about it. It could have jeopardized the entire mission. So I said I did it to calm everybody down and give us a chance to gather more information."

"What did you think would happen to endanger the mission?"

"I was afraid Command would just shut us down and send us home," Gold answered, "especially if—" but she stopped herself.

"Especially if what?" Stanton pressed.

Gold grimaced and looked down. "Especially if they heard fear in your voice."

That stung Stanton.

You don't get to be first, Ferguson had told him once, *because they know you're not fearless. You don't have to be fearless to be the second guy, but you'd damn well better be fearless if you're gonna be the first man on Mars.*

"I— I don't think they would have heard any fear," Stanton stammered back.

"Maybe not," Gold replied. "But they would have heard concern and might have misinterpreted it."

Stanton didn't say anything.

"That's what makes you such a good captain, John," said Gold. "You care about your crew. Even the late addition, government mole, ice princess."

Stanton looked up and smiled at her self deprecating description.

"You care, John," she repeated. "That's what makes you the perfect man for this rescue mission."

Stanton looked Gold in the eye. He was about to say 'Thanks, Cassie,' when Lin walked in.

"I thought I heard your voice, Captain," she said. "I thought you might want to know how Daniel—I mean, Commander Mtumbe—is doing."

"I do, Lieutenant," Stanton smiled. "How is he?"

Lin shrugged. "Well, he's not up and dancing just yet, but he seems more comfortable."

"Well, that's something," said Stanton.

"Hopefully it means he's getting better," said Lin, "and not that he's almost, that is, I mean—"

Lin bit back the words.

"I know what you mean," said Stanton. "We'll just have to wait and hope."

"I hope you burn in hell!" Rusakova screamed from Petrov's room.

Stanton, Gold, and Lin looked at each other then jumped up and ran across the hallway to Petrov's room.

Petrov was standing up and was shaking the figurines over his head. "We must not anger them further, Oksana!" he was pleading. "Our fates are in their hands."

"Damn them!" Rusakova yelled at him, oblivious to the others who had arrived. "And damn you, Aleksandr Ivanovich Petrov!"

"They are angry now, Oksana! I hope you are happy. I hope you are prepared for what will happen next!"

"What will happen next, Aleksandr?! What will your imaginary spirits do to us next, eh?"

And this time when the lights went out, they couldn't blame a sandstorm.

59

"Roll call!" shouted Stanton.

"Lin!" responded the lieutenant.

But that was the only response. Footsteps could be heard running toward the rest of the station. Stanton hoped it was Gold or Rusakova running to switch on the emergency power. But he had a bad feeling in the pit of his stomach this time.

Before he could think of anything else, he felt a hand over his mouth and lips pressed against his ear. Gold's hair and the smell of her skin folded against him as she placed her other hand under his arm and pulled him back toward the commissary.

"Trust me," she whispered.

He did. He allowed himself to be pulled out of the hallway.

"That's the other thing I wanted to talk to you about," Gold whispered into his ear again, the softness of hair almost too distracting. "Someone stole my gun, remember?"

Stanton nodded, even though no one could see. He did

remember. And it had to be one of the four people out there in the dark. If it was Mtumbe, he was no threat in his current condition. If it was Lin, Stanton trusted her enough not to worry too much—although he couldn't think of why would she do something so out of character. If it was Rusakova, that would be bad. Her patience had worn thin and her emotions were right at the surface. The only thing that could have been worse was if Petrov had stolen it.

"Don't worry," whispered Gold. "I have another one."

Stanton heard her rack the slide, loading a cartridge into the chamber. It wasn't a sound Stanton had heard a lot, but it wasn't something he was completely unfamiliar with. It was a distinctive noise, and not a quiet one, especially in the silence of a pitch black space station. So he was absolutely certain the next noise he heard was the slide of a second gun being racked out in the hallway. Directly outside the commissary. Where Petrov's room was.

The next sound was accompanied by the muzzle flash as the gun from the hallway was fired into the commissary, directly at him and Gold.

There was no time to react, so by the time he wondered if he'd be hit, he knew he hadn't. He then wondered, first, whether Gold had been hit, and second, if she hadn't, whether the bullet had breeched the station wall.

The second question was answered by the fact that no blast wall was descending to seal off the commissary. The first question was answered when Gold fired back.

60

The muzzle flash lit up Gold's determined, yet surprisingly calm countenance. The sound of the blasts echoed off the metal commissary walls. Stanton always forgot how loud the discharge of a firearm was. The next sounds were what he had been so relieved not to hear with the first shot: a scream of pain and a whoosh of air.

"Hold your fire!" shouted Lin as she ran down the hallway from the control room with a floodlight. It lit a well of approximately one meter diameter almost like daylight. She stopped in the center of the corridor, right between the commissary and Petrov's room, and right between the two shooters: Gold and Rusakova.

Rusakova sat on Petrov's bed, the gun extended in her still shaking hands. Her eyes were as wide as saucers, abject terror on her face.

Petrov sat behind her, the figurines still grasped in his tightly coiled hands, his eyes skyward, and a dark, gushing gunshot wound in his neck.

Directly behind him, in the wall, was a bullet hole,

which had fragmented the brittle station wall into a half-meter wide gash. It whistled as their air supply raced out into the thinner Martian atmosphere.

"The ghosts were coming for us," said Rusakova without blinking. "Aleksandr said they were coming for us."

Just then the power snapped back on. Although that ordinarily would have been a reason for relief, Stanton jumped up and shouted, "No!"

But it was too late. The alarm went off and the blast wall smashed down, sealing off Rusakova inside Petrov's small room. By the time they figured out how to raise the wall again, or got outside to patch the hole, she would be asphyxiated.

Stanton pounded on the wall, yelling, "Oksana! Aleksandr!" But it was no use. Lin and Gold stayed back while their captain exhausted himself against the blast wall. Then he turned and glowered at Gold.

"Did you really have to shoot?"

"Do you think she would have stopped with just one shot if I hadn't?" Gold replied.

Stanton didn't care what the answer to that was. He'd just lost two more crew members.

That reminded him. "Mtumbe," he murmured.

Lin dropped the now redundant flashlight and sprinted into his cabin. A moment later, she ran back into the commissary, her normally composed countenance in complete disbelief.

"He's gone!"

61

"Gone?" shouted Stanton. "What do you mean he's gone?"

Lin cocked her head at the captain. "I mean he is no longer there."

Stanton got a hold of himself. "Right. I know what you meant. I just don't understand how."

Lin nodded. "Neither do I, but it is the truth."

"Let's take a look," suggested Gold and the three remaining crew members walked to the sleeping berth in question.

When they reached Mtumbe's room, Stanton put out an arm to hold Lin back. "Did you touch anything when you came in before?"

She frowned. "Yes. When he wasn't in his bed, I came in and threw everything aside looking for him. I pulled back his sheets. I looked under the cot. I opened the closet door. I even checked in the dresser drawer. I was stupid, I know, but I guess I wasn't thinking clearly."

"You weren't stupid," Gold reassured her. "You were

looking for your friend."

"So what could have happened?" Stanton asked the group.

"Most likely, he got up and wandered off in the darkness," Gold suggested. "He was probably disoriented from the infection and didn't know where he was or what he was doing."

"Agreed," said Stanton. "Any other possibilities?"

They all thought for several moments. Finally, Lin said, "Well, ..." but then she stopped herself. "No, never mind."

Stanton shook his head. "No, go ahead, Lieutenant. There are no stupid ideas here. It's a brainstorming session."

Lin grimaced. "It is stupid, I assure you." She shrugged. "It's just that I can't help think of what happened to Dekker and what Petrov said about *rusalkas.*"

Gold raised her eyebrows, but didn't say anything. Instead she looked sideways at Stanton. Lin couldn't help but notice.

"See, I told you it was stupid," Lin said. "I'm sorry I even mentioned it."

But Stanton shook his head. "No, no. It's good to voice these things. If it'll make you feel better, I had a similar thought."

Gold's eyebrows went up again. "You think he was body snatched by a Russian ghost?"

Stanton shook his head. "Not exactly. Petrov said that happened after they die, and I'm still hoping he's alive. Petrov told me he was trying to take the evil spirits away from Daniel by handlings those figurines. He said he wasn't long for living. And he was right. I was thinking that if he was right about taking the evil spirits away from Mtumbe, that might explain how Daniel could have gone from so bad just a few hours ago to well enough to get up and wander away in the darkness."

He grinned at Lin. "So you're not the only stupid one."

"That gives me some solace," Lin replied with a soft smile.

"Can I make a more constructive suggestion?" Gold asked.

"Of course," replied Stanton. "No ghosts involved?"

"I don't know," Gold said. "Why don't we see if ghosts get picked up by surveillance cameras. Didn't you say they were all up and running now, Lin?"

Lin's eyes brightened. "Yes, they are."

"So," continued Gold, "we could review the tapes for any sign of what happened to Mtumbe, including seeing him wander around."

"I'll check the tapes!" Lin practically yelled.

"And I'll search the station for any sign of him," Stanton said. "Gold, you should check the ship, See if he may have stumbled into there. If he's delusional, I don't want him to try drive the ship through the station wall."

"Agreed," replied Gold.

Stanton's face looked the most determined it had since they'd left Earth six months earlier. "We need to find Daniel. Go to your assigned tasks, then we meet back at the comm center in twenty minutes."

62

Stanton began at the farthest end of the station as Gold and Lin hurried in the opposite direction to their destinations. He started with the commissary, checking every cupboard and under every table and chair.

Next he crossed the corridor and checked the crew cabins. Dekker's. Gold's. His own. Lin's. Rusakova's. And a double check of Mtumbe's. Nothing.

He stared at Petrov's sealed room and realized Mtumbe might have stumbled in there. If so, it was too late to help him. Stanton shook the idea from his head.

"Keep looking," he told himself.

Next was the communications center. That was quick work, there being nowhere really to hide.

Then down the hall to the command center and Lin. "Any luck?" he asked her.

"Not yet," she shrugged. "I'll keep looking."

"Comm me if you find anything."

"Yes, Captain," and she turned her attention back to the screen she was examining.

Next Stanton worked his way to the west airlock. He couldn't see the place without thinking about how Dekker had died there. And how his body had disappeared. Just like Mtumbe's.

He shook his head again. "No such thing as ghosts," he tried to tell himself. "At least not on Mars."

He pretended not to think about the seven crew members who had died before them and where their souls might have ended up. He'd read once that ghosts were the souls of those who either didn't realize they were dead, perhaps from some sudden accident, or those who knew they were dead but couldn't make it to the next world. Were souls that died on another planet able to make it to the afterlife? And if not, wouldn't they have no choice but to haunt the place they died in?

Again Stanton shook his head. The thoughts were coming too fast now, crowding out his goal: finding Mtumbe. A quick check confirmed he wasn't in the west airlock bay.

On to the entrance to the south equipment bay, and past the sick bay. The blast wall was still down. Stanton wondered what it looked like in there. Had they just overlooked Dekker's body? Was it really just under something, drying out, rotting, mummifying in the Martian air? And what had happened to the antibiotics that had worked so well for Mtumbe and then seemed to abandon him completely?

Daniel. Must find Daniel.

The only area left was the entry bay. Again no sign of Mtumbe. On a hunch Stanton checked the spacesuits but none were missing. Mtumbe hadn't left the station for a sleep-Marswalk.

Stanton pressed the airlock pad and passed through into the ship.

"Gold?" he called out into the half-lit bridge. "Are you here?"

Gold stepped out from the rear quarters of the ship. "Right here, Captain." Then she held her hands palms up. "No sign of him. He's not on the ship."

"He's not in the station either," Stanton replied. "And obviously those can't both be true. So one of us must have missed him."

Stanton sat down in his pilot's chair. "Let's comm Lin and see if she found anything on the video."

Instinctively he passed his hand over the command glass to set up the comm link, but then remembered the ship's comm system was down. But they were about to notice bigger problems.

"Right," Stanton realized as soon as he did it. "This won't work."

He reached for the personal comm link on his suit collar, but Gold stopped him.

"Wait," she said, holding out a hand. "Look at the command glass."

Stanton did, but he didn't recognize what he saw. The usual icons and charts and information screens were scrambled and nonsensical.

"What the hell?" he said, standing up to get a better look at it.

"Looks like the poltergeist got onto the ship too," said Gold dryly.

"Don't even joke about that," Stanton said. "This is too damn serious. If the ship's computer is down, we may be stuck here for eighteen months whether we like it or not, waiting for the next rescue ship."

"Let's hope they have better luck than we've had," said Gold.

"Let's hope we have better luck than the first crew had," Stanton answered.

"Too late," joked Gold. When Stanton didn't laugh, she stepped over to the control glass. "Maybe it's some sort of hardware problem," she suggested. "Crossed wires or something simple."

Stanton shook his head. "Nothing's been simple so far. We're down to three crew members—"

"Four," Gold interrupted. "Don't give up on Daniel just yet."

Stanton smiled. He needed that. "Thanks, Gold."

She smiled too. "Call me Cassie," she said. "No one calls me Cassie."

She stepped up to him and laid a strong, soft hand on his chest. "I don't know how this is going to end, but I wouldn't want to be anywhere else right now than with you, John Stanton."

She leaned up and kissed him on the cheek.

For a moment Stanton just looked at her. Then he kissed her on the mouth. She kissed back, hard.

They kissed longer than they should have under the circumstances, but not long enough. When their lips finally parted, reluctantly, Gold laid her head on Stanton's chest. He leaned down and kissed her hair.

"Let's find Daniel, fix the ship, and get the hell out of here," he said.

"Aye aye, Captain," Gold replied as she lifted her head

and stepped away.

Stanton pressed his comm link. "Lin? Lin, do you copy?"

There was no reply.

"Lin, do you copy?"

Still no reply.

Stanton looked back toward the station. "I've got a bad feeling about this."

63

Stanton and Gold hurried through the airlock and directly to the command center. But they were too late.

Lin was hanging heavily from a metal support beam, a thick communications cable around her throat, her toes just off the ground.

"Holy shit!" shouted Stanton and he rushed in to lift her body upward.

Gold didn't say anything. She just stood and stared.

"Help me get her down," Stanton said as he held the body aloft, slackening the cable. Gold grabbed the chair from the control desk and stood on it to untie the cord. The metal wire was too thick to cut, and the support beam was just out of her reach, so Gold was forced to insert her fingers between the cord and Lin's flesh to undo the knot around her comrade's neck.

Stanton recalled learning that in the heyday of hanging, the poor unfortunate's death was usually caused by a broken neck from the fall through the gallows trapdoor. But strangulation could cause the death as well and that was clearly the case here. Lin suffered the broken eye blood vessels and swollen tongue indicative of the painful process of the brain being deprived of blood and oxygen.

Once the knot was finally undone, they laid Lin on the floor and cast aside the cord. Stanton sat back on his heels and sighed.

"This doesn't make sense," he said.

"Maybe she was distraught over Mtumbe?" Gold suggested, not very convincingly.

Stanton shrugged. "Maybe," he said. "Let's check the video. Maybe she saw something overwhelmingly distressing."

The monitor had gone into sleep mode, but when they slid a hand over the glass a paused image popped up onto the screen. It was of Mtumbe, but not with nefarious spirits carting away his body, or of him writhing on the ground in Petrov's cabin as his lungs exploded from the onslaught of Martian air through the bullet hole, or even of him sneaking out through the south equipment bay in a hijacked spacesuit.

It was an image from their first day there. He was beaming that disarming smile of his and glancing toward Lin.

"That's a nice picture of him," Gold said. "Maybe she was distraught over him being, well, missing anyway."

Stanton examined the image on the screen. He wasn't convinced. "Maybe, but it hardly seems like something you'd just kill yourself over."

"Well, we've all been under a lot of stress," Gold suggested. "Maybe she finally snapped."

"Petrov snapped," said Stanton. "Lin was very unsnappy."

He leaned forward and examined the image carefully.

"Where is this? The entry bay?"

Gold reached out to the control glass. "Let's zoom out and see."

She tapped the glass and the image pulled back to show not only Mtumbe and Lin, but the entire crew, even Dekker, assembled in the entry bay. They were all wearing their travel suits. It must have been right after they disembarked.

As Stanton studied the image, he realized something. "Wasn't Petrov in the entry bay when he first said he saw a ghost?"

Gold shrugged. "I don't know. I was on the roof with you." She gave a nervous cough. "And I was kind of out of it. He thought I'd been possessed."

Stanton shook his head. "You just had too much oxygen and not enough experience. Your first spacewalk can be overwhelming."

He thought for a second. "Rusakova and I found him hiding on the ship. He said he'd been in the entry bay when he saw a ghost in the control glass. Reflected in the control glass."

Stanton returned his attention to the image on the monitor. "Weren't you going to tell me something about that 'Croatoan' word. Didn't you say it was related to the carving in the catacomb somehow?"

Gold was surprised by the sudden shift in conversation. "Er, yes. Um, I learned about it in one of my college American history courses. One of the theories of what happened to the colonists was that they sought refuge with or were captured by one of the nearby Native American tribes. That theory received support from an archaeological dig almost four hundred years later that found a ring with that same horse and X design on it. Apparently that was the coat of arms of the leader of the colonists. The ring was found in the middle of a Native American settlement from the same time and area."

Stanton nodded. "Leader of the colonists, huh?" He looked at the image again, then knelt down and started examining Lin's neck.

"What are you doing?" Gold asked, kneeling beside him.

"There," whispered Stanton, pointing to the purple bruising around the neck. "Look at that."

"What?" asked Gold, not whispering.

"The bruising," Stanton whispered again

"Well, of course there was bruising," Gold succumbed to the whispering. "She was strangled to death by a cord."

"So why are there fingerprint bruises?" Stanton illustrated the shape of the bruise by placing a finger against one of the faint purple circles above the dark, straight bruise from the cord.

"Did I cause that when I undid the cord?" whispered Gold.

Stanton shook his head. "No, bruising happens when blood gets pumped into the skin from broken capillaries. Her heart was very much not pumping when you touched her. These are pre-mortem."

He stood up again and pointed at the surveillance image. "Do you see that?"

"That shadow?" Gold confirmed. "Sure. What about it?"

"Doesn't it look like a person's shadow?"

Gold analyzed it critically. "Sure. I guess."

"So who's casting it?" Stanton asked. "Not anyone in

the picture. The lighting is all wrong. Someone else is there."

Gold frowned at the image. "Do you think it's a ghost? Some kind of Martian shadow person?"

Stanton shook his head. "No," he said heavily, slowly rising from his crouch over the monitor. "It's no ghost."

He turned and looked around the room, up and down, at the ceiling and floor, and all the seam joints in the metal walls.

He clenched his fists. "You can come out now."

"Who?" asked Gold, taking a step toward him and looking around as well for some idea of what Stanton was talking about. "Mtumbe?"

Stanton put an arm around Gold's waist and waited. "No," he growled. "Not Mtumbe."

Then one of the metal wall joints behind them started to shake. They turned and watched as a section of the wall popped out and slid over. Then, from within the station's walls, stepped a large, tired, desperate man, Gold's first gun displayed in his meaty hand.

"I wondered if you were gonna figure it out, Junior."

64

Stanton just stared at him. Although he'd figured it out, he still couldn't quite believe it.

"Agent Cassandra Gold," Stanton said, "may I introduce Captain Bruce Ferguson, leader of the first manned colony on Mars."

"Pleased to meet you, ma'am," Ferguson grinned. He had a deep baritone voice, his barrel chest practically shook when he spoke, and it almost sounded like he wasn't insane.

Gold didn't respond. Instead her hand started to slide up her hip toward her gun.

"Uh, uh, uh," warned Ferguson, raising his own gun from the low ready. "Don't be stupid. I've been watching you and I know you're not stupid."

"Where have you been this whole time, Ferguson?" asked Stanton. "Not behind that wall there."

"No, Junior, not just behind this wall here." Ferguson nodded toward it but didn't take his eye, or the gun, off of Gold and Stanton. "There's an emergency interior section to this station, in case of something truly catastrophic. You should have known that from the blueprints. It was tiny to start with, really not much more than a small safe room, but I've had nine months to expand it into a self-sufficient station within a station. And I could monitor everything you all did from inside there."

Gold asked the obvious question. "Why?"

"Well, young lady," he started. "I wished no ill to your crew. I just didn't want you to stay either. I was hoping you'd leave after you saw the station abandoned. That's why I carved the word 'Croatoan' in the wall. So you'd think the colony was lost—just like Roanoke—and you'd return home right away."

"Didn't you want to go back to Earth?" Gold pressed.

Ferguson shifted his weight uneasily. "I don't think there's a lot for me back on Earth. Especially after what happened out here."

"What did happen out here, Ferguson?" Stanton asked.

"Those damn engineers, Junior, that's what happened!" His voice rose in anger. "Didn't I always say we couldn't trust those damn pencil pushers who'd never set boot off-planet?"

"You did say that," Stanton agreed.

"They fucked up the food supply ratio calculations," Ferguson explained.

"The what?" Gold asked. When both Stanton and Ferguson looked at her disapprovingly, she defended, "I was a last minute addition to the crew. Sorry I don't know all the lingo."

"The food ratio calculations," Stanton repeated. "The engineers had to figure out how much food the colony would need, then make sure that they could grow enough food to feed everyone for eighteen months."

"It's not like we could run to the store or order a pizza," Ferguson grimaced.

"So they messed up?" Stanton asked.

"Yes, damn them," Ferguson shouted. "Damn them straight to hell. We should have made one of them come with us, then I bet there would have been enough food."

"You ran out of food?" Gold asked.

"Not exactly," Ferguson replied. "It was worse. After about nine months we could tell we were going to run out before the relief crew—you—could arrive."

Stanton understood the ramifications. It was something he'd wondered about, but he knew it would be okay because Ferguson's crew would have already proved the food supply would be adequate. Maybe Ferguson was right about him, that he wasn't really pioneer material.

"So what did you do?" Stanton asked.

"Well, what could we do, Junior?" Ferguson barked back. "We couldn't increase supply so we had to reduce demand."

Gold winced. "Reduce demand?"

Ferguson shrugged. "'Fraid so. I did the calculations myself. With seven crew members, we'd all starve at about ten months. With only six crew members, we'd starve at twelve months. We needed to get down to four crew members to make it until your team arrived."

"So you murdered three of your own crew?" Gold was aghast.

"Of course not, young lady," boomed Ferguson. "I double checked my figures, presented them to the crew, and solicited input on how we would decide who should survive and who not."

"How'd they take that?" Stanton asked, figuring he knew the answer.

"They mutinied," Ferguson replied flatly. "So I killed them. All of them."

Gold blinked at the nonchalant revelation. "You murdered six people?"

Ferguson scowled at her. "Murdered? Not at all. I am the captain of this station. They mutinied. Mutiny is a capital offense—or at least it was. Well, it should be anyway. So no, I didn't murder anyone. I executed mutineers."

"And there was more than enough food for one person," Stanton pointed out.

"Exactly," agreed Ferguson. "So I set out to build my crew a proper burial ground—"

"The catacomb," Gold realized.

"—and a memorial," Ferguson finished.

"The standing stones," said Stanton.

"Of course," Ferguson flashed a disturbing grin. "They may have been traitorous bastards, but they were also brave astronauts and pioneers. They deserved something to honor their service. Besides I needed something to do with my time."

"So when we didn't leave right away," asked Stanton, "you attacked my crew?"

Ferguson frowned at his school mate. "Attacked, Junior? That's a pretty strong word. No, I just tried to convince you to leave. I booby trapped the station door. Then I transmitted an image across the control glass to make you think the station might be haunted by the crew's ghosts. But that didn't work either."

"It kind of worked," Gold murmured. "Petrov believed it."

"Yes, but you didn't leave," answered Ferguson. "So then I had to get more aggressive. So I put out my old spacesuit, the one I'd worn to dig out that mausoleum for my crew. It was ready to give out any minute." He allowed himself a satisfied smile. "And sure enough it did."

"You murdered Dekker!" Gold snarled and took a step toward Ferguson, but he raised the gun slightly and Stanton pulled her back.

"I didn't murder anyone," Ferguson replied. "It was an accident. And anyway, I gave him a decent burial in the mausoleum alongside the others who have died here."

Now they knew what happened to Dekker's body.

"But you still didn't leave," Ferguson lamented. "So I also replaced Commander Mtumbe's antibiotics with vitamin supplements."

Stanton tensed up in anger but he knew not to try anything just yet.

"If you were going to stay we'd need to eliminate four of your crew. Lieutenant Dekker was one, Commander Mtumbe would be two."

"And Petrov and Rusakova made four," Gold calculated.

"So why did you murder Lin?" Stanton demanded.

"Because she caught me," Ferguson laughed. "She was examining the video and spotted me in the background. I was watching her when I realized what she'd found. She was about to comm you so I had to stop her."

Stanton was numb in disbelief.

"We're down to three now," Ferguson observed. "So there's enough food. I don't suppose you'd be willing to stay here under my command?"

Stanton shook his head, "Afraid not, Ferguson."

"Go to hell!" Gold spat.

Ferguson shrugged and let out a deep sigh. "Yes, I suspect I will."

Then he raised the gun and pointed it directly at Stanton's chest.

"Goodbye, Junior," he said and fired.

65

Gold leapt in front of her captain and took the bullet to her shoulder.

Then, before Ferguson could realize he needed to fire another round, Mtumbe shoved aside a second wall panel and jumped Ferguson from behind.

Stanton was still stunned by not being dead. He bent down to check on Gold while Mtumbe and Ferguson smashed into the corner of the comm center, struggling over the gun.

"I'm okay," croaked Gold. "Help Daniel."

Mtumbe was obviously not dead, but he was also still very weak. Once Ferguson overcame the initial shock of being attacked, he regained his wits and raised a foot to Mtumbe's stomach as they struggled. He kicked Mtumbe away, sending him tumbling to the floor. As Mtumbe pushed himself onto all fours, Ferguson stepped up next to him and pressed the gun against his head.

"Goodbye, Commander. I'll bury your body with proper honors."

The sound of a gunshot echoed through the comm

center. Ferguson turned and glared at Stanton. He opened his mouth to say something, then collapsed to the floor—dead.

Gold's shot had pierced his heart.

Stanton looked at his dead mentor, then at his living friend. "You okay, Daniel?"

He flashed that smile of his. "I'm fine, Captain. That antibiotic shot worked. When the lights went out, I felt better enough to try to help. I went to turn the emergency lights on in the control room, but accidentally found an opening to Ferguson's lair. I finally figured out what was going on so I stayed hidden to see what happened next."

"Hello?" Gold called out from the floor. "Gunshot wound here."

"Oh right," Stanton hurried over and helped her sit up. "You okay, Gold?"

She looked at him disapprovingly. He looked uncomfortably at Mtumbe, then relaxed. "You okay, Cassie?"

"I'm okay, John," she answered. Then she leaned over and kissed him on the cheek. "Let's go home."

END

THE DAVID BRUNELLE LEGAL THRILLERS
Presumption of Innocence
Tribal Court
By Reason of Insanity
A Prosecutor for the Defense
Substantial Risk
Corpus Delicti
Accomplice Liability
A Lack of Motive
Missing Witness
Diminished Capacity
Devil's Plea Bargain
Homicide in Berlin
Premeditated Intent
Alibi Defense

THE TALON WINTER LEGAL THRILLERS
Winter's Law
Winter's Chance
Winter's Reason
Winter's Justice
Winter's Duty
Winter's Passion

MAGGIE DEVEREAUX PARANORMAL MYSTERIES
Scottish Rite
Blood Rite
Last Rite

ALSO BY STEPHEN PENNER
The Godling Club
Mars Station Alpha

ABOUT THE AUTHOR

Stephen Penner is an author, artist, and attorney from Seattle.

In addition to writing the Maggie Devereaux Paranormal Mysteries, he is also the author of the David Brunelle Legal Thriller Series, featuring Seattle homicide prosecutor David Brunelle; the Talon Winter Legal Thrillers, starring Tacoma criminal defense attorney Talon Winter; and several stand-alone works.

For more information, please visit *www.stephenpenner.com.*

www.ingramcontent.com/pod-product-compliance
Lightning Source LLC
Chambersburg PA
CBHW051427170626
46809CB00006B/2347